Lilly's Choice

Masters of the Prairie Winds Club
Book Eleven

by Avery Gale

Prologue

DEAN WEST STOOD beside his wife's hospital bed, holding her bruised hand between his own calloused palms and sent up another silent prayer for her recovery. Lilly West was such a force of nature, it was often easy to forget how fragile she was and how quickly life could change. He was certain he'd have nightmares for the rest of his life thinking about what might have happened if she hadn't been wearing her safety belt and been driving the Volvo XC60 SUV they'd bought her less than a month ago. The car's safety rating had been the reason he and his brother, Del had chosen it for her, and now, he was grateful they hadn't listened to her protests about the cost.

"Has she awakened, yet?" Del stepped up along the other side of the bed and ran the backs of his fingers down the side of her battered face. They'd been waiting what seemed like an eternity for her to open her beautiful blue eyes although it had only been a couple of hours.

"No, but she's been more restless in the last few minutes, and the doctor said that would be a sign she was starting to surface." Taking a deep breath, Dean met his brother's gaze and saw the same devastation he felt. Del might have been the first one to see her all those years ago, but they both loved her with everything in them.

There hadn't been a day in the past three and a half decades she hadn't challenged them, but Lilly had never let a single day pass she hadn't taken time to spend with them individually. Even on the rare occasions they'd been separated because of business obligations, he and Del always made certain theirs were the last voices she heard before falling asleep. Today, they planned to make sure theirs were the first she heard when she finally regained consciousness.

"Did you realize tomorrow is the anniversary of the first day we saw her? In so many ways, it feels like yesterday." Leaning closer, Dean whispered, "Come back to us, Darlin', we have a million more ways to show you how much we love you."

LILLY COULD HEAR voices, but they sounded so far away, she had trouble making out the words. Why did everything hurt so much? Damn, even breathing was a battle... who let the sumo wrestler sit on her chest, anyway? *Wouldn't you think someone would notice something like that?*

The only thing she knew was if she'd died, this sure as the angels sing wasn't heaven because there was too much pain... and if she hadn't died and this was a preview of the coming attractions in hell, she needed to think long and hard about fixing whatever she'd done to cause this damned lesson.

Slipping slowly back into oblivion, Lilly felt like she was sliding through a tunnel as events from her life played out around her in a colorful panorama. It was the oddest feeling to watch her life passing in reverse until she found herself seated at a table in a New York bistro that looked wonderfully familiar.

Chapter One

L ILLY GRAHAM FOUGHT the urge to roll her eyes as her sister chattered about everything and nothing. It was no wonder their father had sworn Daisy had been vaccinated with a Victrola needle. Daisy Graham had started talking early and had barely stopped since to take a deep breath. Lilly had tuned her out shortly thereafter because as everyone knew, there was only one topic that was of interest to Daisy, and that was *Daisy*.

"Do you ever wonder what the hell our parents were thinking naming us after flowers?" *Nope, not ever, but I have wondered how they managed to not strangle you.* "Why not saints or Greek goddesses? Seriously, there were so many other options. What did Mom do, go to a garden show or something? Lilly, are you listening to me?" *That's another big negative, sister.* God in heaven, Daisy could talk longer about nothing than anyone Lilly knew, and she often wondered if anyone would notice if Daisy said anything significant... *probably not.*

Tuning out Daisy's monologue which was now focused on how she was going to survive flying home business class on a commercial flight, Lilly let her gaze wander out the restaurant's large front window as two cowboys walked down the sidewalk. No, walked wasn't the right word. They sauntered, although she doubted the two men dressed in dark jeans, crisply pressed white button-down shirts, and boots would describe their walk with that particular verb.

They were obviously brothers, and unless she was missing her guess, they were twins. It was easy to see where some people might mistake them for one another, but even at this distance, she knew she never would. There were distinct differences the casual observer would probably never notice, but she found intriguing in their subtlety. One of the men seemed to sense her stare, and when he lifted his eyes, their gazes locked as if they'd been fused together between one heartbeat and the next. Without looking away, he spoke to his brother who followed his gaze and smiled when he looked her way.

"Good Lord, are you looking at those two cowboys? What are you thinking? You can find men like them at home. We're here to sample new flavors—let's go metro for a change." Daisy's voice had taken on the infuriating haughtiness Lilly found so annoying, and she fought the urge to walk away and not look back.

Lilly had been looking forward to a little downtime, but when her much-needed break turned into a shopping trip with Daisy, the anticipation had turned to dread. Spending time with Daisy was always a poisonous mixture of annoyance and exhaustion and always seemed to leave Lilly comatose for days after returning home.

Looking up as the two cowboys walked confidently through the small restaurant toward her, Lilly smiled to herself for the first time in weeks—suddenly, the next few days blossomed with potential. *Damn Skippy, with a little luck, perhaps this trip would turn out to be more than an exercise in survival.*

DEL WEST WAS proud as hell of himself for not stumbling when his eyes locked onto the most beautiful woman he'd ever seen. Something about her seemed vaguely familiar, but he was sure they'd never met—there wasn't a chance in hell he'd have forgotten her.

"Change of plans, brother. We're meeting a woman instead." Even to his own ears, Del's voice sounded rough with a flood of desire that had nearly taken him to his knees. He'd never had such an intense reaction to a woman. Everything about her was absolute perfection, and his soul was screaming *'mine'* so loud, he barely heard Dean's response over the din.

"A woman? You're blowing off the reason we're here to meet a woman?" Del knew his brother would follow his gaze, and when he heard Dean's muttered curse, he chuckled. "Who is she? I've seen her picture in a magazine somewhere, but I can't remember where."

"Fucking hell. No wonder she looks familiar. With her face and that sexy smile, it's only reasonable she's a model. We're probably wasting our time, but let's ask her if she'll have dinner with us tonight." He didn't intend to miss the business meeting they'd been planning for months, but he knew the chances their paths would cross again in a city this size was slim to none. Giving her a sly smile, Del led Dean into the posh restaurant. Waving off the maître d', they walked straight to the table where the woman sat with another woman who was chattering like it was her damned job.

Since they'd both removed their hats at the door, Del ran his hand through his short-cropped hair, more out of habit than necessity, as he nodded at the beauty who was eyeing him with barely restrained lust.

"I'm Del West, and this is my brother Dean. We were wondering if you would join us for dinner this evening." Her dark blue eyes widened as her pupils dilated, and Del felt a measure of satisfaction knowing she wasn't unaffected by the two of them. She glanced between the two men as her companion huffed out a frustrated sigh. The gorgeous woman his soul was screaming belonged to him rolled her eyes at the other woman's snort of derision.

"I don't understand it. You were just sitting there, staring out the damned window while I'm trying to talk to you, and two... not one, but *two* men walk in off the street to ask you out. Un-fucking-believable." Pushing her chair back, the second woman stood quickly and took a step away from the table. "I'm going to freshen up before we go back to the hotel's spa." Before she walked away, she turned back to the woman she'd been sitting with and rolled her eyes. "Don't forget the Carlson's party this evening, Lilly. Mom and Dad will be pissed if you disappoint Mary Beth."

Lilly. So, their angel was named after a beautiful flower—how appropriate. In his peripheral vision, Del saw Dean grin. They'd also been invited to Robert and Mary Beth Carlson's party but hadn't planned to attend—until now. Neither Del nor Dean had been able to take their eyes off Lilly as the other woman huffed an unladylike snort before stomping away.

"I'm sorry if our interruption annoyed your friend, but I don't regret the interruption itself." He wasn't about to apologize for asking out the most beautiful woman he'd ever seen or for ignoring the unpleasant mess she'd eaten lunch with.

"She isn't my friend."

Del felt his own eyes widen in surprise when he heard a familiar twang in her soft voice. So, the lovely lady is a Texan? Isn't that convenient?

"Daisy is my sister. We're visiting the city for a few days before I return home and she settles back in for another semester at the University of Texas."

He gave her a smile he hoped made it look like he was appropriately impressed with her sister's academic pursuits because if her attitude was any indication, Daisy probably wasn't a stellar student.

"Where's home, Darlin'?" Dean West could turn his southern drawl on and off like a light switch. Del knew his brother as well as he knew himself and wanted to chuckle at Dean's shameless flirting. He'd asked the question they both wanted answered, and he'd given her an enormous clue about their own home state. Lilly's smile told him she hadn't missed the less than subtle hint.

"Houston originally but I've been living in Dallas for the past few years. I've been pursuing a modeling career, so I travel a lot."

A surge of something akin to possessiveness moved through Del like a lightning storm, and he had to make a concerted effort to refocus his attention on their conversation. Thinking about other men looking at Lilly's picture, lusting after her made his vision wash with red for a few seconds before he pulled himself back from the edge of anger.

"Well, we're practically neighbors. I can't believe we've never met." Dean took a step closer to Lilly, and Del hoped like hell his brother wasn't moving too quickly. The last thing he wanted was to scare her away. "We live in Austin most of the year, but we keep a place in Houston as well."

Del wanted to roll his eyes because they kept the condo in Houston specifically, so they had a place to stay when they found time to visit their favorite kink club, but those visits had become less frequent over the past year.

Del had been more restless the past year than he'd ever remembered being, and he hadn't been sure why until he'd locked eyes with Lilly. At twenty-eight, they were far from confirmed bachelors, and they'd always discussed marrying young, in hopes they'd still be active enough when they had grandchildren to keep up with them. Despite those discussions, with very few of their friends married or even in committed relationships, it hadn't occurred to Del a woman was the answer to the riddle that had plagued him for so many months.

"Daisy was right about the party. I can't disappoint the Carlsons. Your invitation is tempting... *very* tempting, but I'm afraid I'll have to decline." Del could hear the regret in her voice, and that pleased him more than it should.

"Perhaps I can offer a compromise. We've also been invited to the Carlson's this evening, we'd love to act as your escorts." Del saw her breathing hitch and knew she wanted to say yes. *Be brave, Beautiful.*

"We might even be able to duck out early and take a carriage ride around the park, it's amazing at night." What Dean hadn't said was how perfectly she would fit between them during the ride. It would be cool enough, they'd be able to snuggle with her under a blanket. He could hardly wait to find out if her ruby lips tasted as sweet as they looked. Lilly's eyes darkened again as they darted between the two men. She seemed to be considering her words carefully, but Del had the impression that wasn't her nature. There was a wild energy surrounding her Del found himself almost magnetically drawn to even though it was usually something he avoided. *Hell, dealing with Dean is enough chaos for anyone.*

"Daisy was planning to attend the party with friends who are also here shopping... and I must admit, being the fifth wheel doesn't sound very appealing, but I'm not certain being the third..."

"We'll never make you feel like an outsider, Lilly, so don't start with the third wheel comments." Stepping past his brother, Del leaned closer and slowly brushed the long, chestnut waves of her hair over her shoulder so he could whisper against the sensitive shell of her ear. "Being between the two of us will be a pleasure unlike any other, Beautiful. Be brave. Say yes." He smiled to himself when she shuddered and leaned close enough he could feel the warm breath of her gasp caress his neck.

There was something almost magnetic about the energy surrounding Lilly, but Del sensed there was also a deep well of sensuality he'd bet was untapped. He and Dean could show her more pleasure than she'd ever imagined possible if she'd give them the chance. Watching her blossom as she learned the power of her own sexuality would bring him as much joy as the sex itself.

"Yes."

Her breathless reply was music to his ears, but he didn't get to relish the feeling for long since Daisy chose that moment to reappear at the table. Del didn't care they were in a crowded eatery in one of the most metropolitan cities in the world. Knowing they had an audience hadn't bothered him until Daisy's voice shattered the sensual, promise-filled silence that had followed Lilly's answer.

"Lilly Graham, I swear to all that's holy I can't leave you alone for a minute. Come on, we are not missing our spa appointment because you want to be the cream cheese filling in a hick-bologna sandwich." As if the grating tone of her voice wasn't enough to make him homicidal, the young woman's public insult to her sister was the last straw. Standing up, Del focused his attention fully on Daisy.

"Stop."

His one-word command made her mouth snap shut with such force, he wondered if she'd chipped her perfectly polished teeth. Hell, her parents had probably funded all the woman's dental work, hoping one of the dental professionals would wire her damned mouth shut.

"Your sister has done nothing to earn your rabid attitude. If you are genuinely curious why she attracts people, you'd do well to imitate rather than criticize her." A man sitting at a nearby table snorted a laugh he made a pathetically lame attempt to hide with a quick cough, and a woman seated to Daisy's right gave him a double thumbs up worthy of the best Southerner which he found damned amusing considering the dress she was wearing probably cost more than his first truck.

Turning back to Lilly, Del was pleased to see Dean holding her small hand between his much larger ones—the comforting gesture appeared to be settling her. It was situations like this one that reminded Del why he'd always believed sharing a woman with his brother would be in everyone's best interest.

Together, they could provide so much *more...* hell, a man could only pay so much attention when a significant portion of his blood migrated south. It took two men to keep up with most of the women they found interesting. In his experience, the best sex was always with the brightest women—where was the reward in earning the trust of a woman if she surrendered to every man she met? It was also why the club had lost its allure. Negotiated scenes with subs whose names he'd already forgotten before he hit the door had become meaningless. Turning back to Lilly, Del saw nothing but gratitude in her eyes.

"Where are you staying, Beautiful?"

"St. Regis, Room five-twenty." There was a twinkle of mischief in her eyes now, and Del knew she'd just given them information she didn't ordinarily share with dates, let alone virtual strangers. Most women preferred to meet men in the lobby, and he was grateful she'd trusted him enough to reveal her room number. Pulling a business card from his wallet, Del carefully noted both his and Dean's cell numbers on the back before handing it to her.

"We'll pick you up at seven." He saw the question in her eyes and smoothed his fingers down the side of her face. "We are staying across the street at The Peninsula Hotel, so we'll walk over and arrange for a car to pick us up there—let's spend a few minutes chatting before we're forced to socialize." He hoped his smile didn't look as horny as he felt—hell, just thinking about being alone with her was testing his control.

"Call us when you get back to your room, so we know you are safe, Darlin'. We're headed to a meeting, but we'll be thinking about you." Damn, sometimes Dean was a fucking genius. They'd just purchased the newest mobile phones and were pleased she'd be able to contact them no matter where they were. They'd also get her number since he was certain she'd also have one of the new mobiles that were finally making their way to public use. *Well done, brother.*

Chapter Two

L ILLY WAS TRYING very hard to keep from strangling her younger sister. Daisy's constant chatter had been bad enough, but the persistent whining—because Lilly was going to the party with two hot men rather than tagging along with her kid sister's group—was too much. When Lilly started fantasizing about how it would feel to push Daisy out of the Towne Car the hotel had graciously sent to shuttle them from one wing of the building to another, it was time to speak up.

"You just as well stop grumbling because I'm not changing my mind. Why should I? You'll ditch me as soon as we step through the Carlson's door, and we both know it. You claim I'm the one who attracts men, but you are the one who is always surrounded by a posse no man wants to wade through." Lilly took a deep breath and tried to pull back her escalating frustration. Damn it all to hell in a pair of hot pants, anyway.

Lilly knew better than to let Daisy get to her. It wasn't like this was new—hell, she'd been dealing with Daisy's jealousy since her younger sister learned to talk… and Lilly was sure Daisy uttered her first words in the delivery room… *probably bitching about the lighting not being perfect for her complexion or her hair being mussed.* Taking a deep breath, hoping the infusion of oxygen would clear some of the frustration from her brain, Lilly refocused on Daisy.

"I work. That's it. I work. The only thing I do other than work or travel for work is when I let you talk me into one of these shopping trips... trips which always seem to coincide with your friends being in town." When Daisy started to protest, Lilly held up her hand to silence the rebuttal. "I don't want to hear it. I'm going to the party with Del and Dean... *Period*. The subject is not open for discussion. You can be excited for me, or you can alienate me with your jealousy, the choice is yours to make." Just as she finished speaking, the door opened, and the hotel's valet helped her step from the car.

Without looking back, Lilly walked into the hotel with her head held high. She could hear her sister's heels clicking on the marble floor before falling silent once she'd reached the thick carpet near the small alcove where the elevators were located. Daisy managed to slip into the elevator before the doors closed, and Lilly wanted to curse being a captive audience because once her sister set out on a path—no matter how destructive—she rarely backed down.

"You don't know anything about them. They could be stalkers; your meeting might not have been as *accidental* as you believe. They could be like that jerk you dated in high school. Have you ever thought about that?" Daisy was nothing if not hell-bent on burning down anything remotely good in Lilly's life and resurrecting everything bad. As the beloved youngest child, Daisy had always managed to manipulate their parents in ways Lilly wouldn't have dared try. There were only five years between them in age, but they were miles apart in personality.

"I'm not stupid, Daisy. I've already checked them out." And she had. While her sister had been enjoying an hour-long massage, Lilly had been busy researching. She'd called a friend in Dallas who worked for a private investigation firm, knowing the company Suzy worked for would have access to information that wouldn't be found in the public record. When she'd heard Suzy's whistle, Lilly wondered if the news was going to be incredibly good or alarmingly bad.

Lilly met Suzy the first week she'd lived in Dallas. They lived in the same building and often found themselves in the building's gym at the same time. They'd hit it off right away, and Lilly was grateful for Suzy's friendship. Lilly didn't have a lot of female friends because so many of the women she met were put off by her physical appearance.

She might have always assumed she was the problem, but a few had been daring enough to tell her they were intimidated and felt they'd never have a chance picking up a man if she were along. The accusations had stung because she'd heard the same complaint from her own sister. Fortunately for her, Suzy was comfortable in her own skin, and the two of them had become fast friends. Suzy checked on Lilly's condo when she was traveling, and Lilly had acted as a decoy on Suzy's stakeouts on several occasions. She'd been delighted because for once her looks had helped solidify a friendship rather than undermining it.

"Those two are hot, my friend. Really hot... and loaded. They took a relatively small inheritance from their grandfather and started their own shipping business." Suzy whistled again, her husky chuckle coming over the line. "Let's just say money will never be an issue, okay? Now, for something a bit more interesting. These fellas don't work alone if you know what I mean. They're known for sharing more than a river mansion in Austin. Why they run a billion-dollar shipping business from inland is an interesting question, but back to the ménage thing. They are rumored to frequent kink clubs... really exclusive clubs where memberships can run in the six-figure range and talking will tank your entire life."

Suzy cut their conversation short when she got another call, and Lilly sent up a silent prayer her friend had gotten a tip about a missing child she'd been tracking for several weeks. The little boy was last seen with his stepmother who'd repeatedly denied any knowledge of his disappearance.

Lilly refocused her attention on her sister standing ramrod straight across the opulent elevator, staring at her. The look was one Lilly recognized all too well... her sister had obviously been talking to her and was growing impatient with Lilly's lack of response. Before she could open her mouth to speak, the doors slid open, signaling they'd arrived on their floor. Lilly was exhausted and had no plans to continue beating a dead horse as her grandfather used to say. There were several people in the sitting room outside the elevator, and the last thing Lilly wanted was to have her picture snapped by some tourist while she argued with her kid sister.

Heading the short distance to her room, Lilly called over her shoulder, "I'll see you at the party. I'm looking forward to seeing you in your new dress. You always look stunning in red." Daisy paused just long enough for Lilly to push her key into the lock and open the door. Glancing to her side, she saw the smile on Daisy's face and wanted to roll her eyes at how easily her sister could be distracted. Happy her compliment had hit its mark, Lilly stepped into the cool room and kicked off her shoes as she leaned back against the door and sighed.

She was supposed to spend the next few days in New York before returning to Texas, but exhaustion was beginning to weigh her down. *God knows shopping with Daisy is anything but relaxing.* Shaking her head, Lilly wondered what she'd been thinking when she agreed to let her sister horn in on what was supposed to be a break. *I thought it would be a good way to unwind after three weeks on the road... and that's exactly what I need to do.*

Pushing away from the door, Lilly pulled Del West's card and her phone from her oversized purse before tossing the leather bag aside. Pouring herself a glass of wine, she settled into one of the chairs facing the balcony and entered Del and Dean's numbers in her small address book before dialing Del's number. She'd promised to let them know when she'd returned to her hotel, and she wanted to make sure she'd done it before lying down for a quick nap.

"Lilly?"

"Yes. I wanted to let you know I've returned to my room and plan to rest a bit... I'm having trouble keeping my eyes open." The spa had been too sedate, the tranquil setting and soothing ambiance nearly melting her into a puddle rather than recharging her.

"When did you last eat, Beautiful?" Del's question was spoken quietly, but with a tone of authority Lilly didn't even consider discounting.

"Does she need us to call her later to make sure she's awakened? Or I could blow off the rest of this meeting and go watch over her personally." She could hear Dean's teasing words and knew he must be standing close to his brother.

"Damn it, Dean, stop monkeying around and pay attention to whatever what's his name is saying." Del sounded like he was fighting amusement which made Lilly giggle.

"What's his name? You don't know the man's name,

and you're worried about Dean missing the presentation?"

"Dean's the numbers guy. He should be listening."

"And Del is bossy. I'm much more affable, something I expect you'll sort out soon enough." Lilly giggled when she heard what sounded suspiciously like a growl from Del.

"Pay attention! There is a lot at stake here."

"Later, Darlin'." Even without being able to see them, she could sense Dean had moved away from his brother from the shift in the energy and background noise alone.

"I'm sorry I interrupted your meeting. I just wanted to let you know I'm back in my room. It was a very long afternoon, but I'm looking forward to seeing you." A crisp rap sounded on the door of Lilly's small suite, and she sighed... so much for resting. "I have to go, there's someone at the door."

"Eat something, Beautiful. We'll see you soon." Lilly couldn't help but smile at Del's concern for her well-being. She opened the door when the man on the other side held up his hotel identification for her to see. He walked briskly into the room to set a large tray on the table. "For you, Miss. There is a note on the tray." She must have looked confused because he smiled, shaking his head when she finally came back to her senses and reached for her purse. "No, ma'am. The gentleman who ordered for you has already taken care of everything."

Opening the note, Lilly smiled when she saw Del and Dean had anticipated her need for a snack and arranged for its delivery before she'd even known she'd need it. Perhaps some things she read in romance novels weren't so far off the mark after all.

DEL LEANED BACK in the leather chair, smiling to himself. He'd gotten her phone number and confirmed she'd given him the correct room number—hell, the timing couldn't have been any more perfect. It wasn't that he didn't understand why women gave men phony room numbers until they could check them out because he did—but that didn't mean he wasn't pleased to learn Lilly hadn't tried to blow smoke up their asses earlier today.

He knew she and her sister had spa appointments, but that hadn't kept her from checking on them. Unfortunately for her, Lilly had called an agency owned by a friend and fellow Dom. Dante Radison had entered alerts in his database for the Doms at the club they all belonged to, and when Dean and Del's names popped up, he'd had a chat with the employee who'd taken the call. Suzy Quintara had been very helpful once she'd understood the penalties for misuse of company resources.

Del offered to pay for the background information she'd given Lilly, hoping it would help her friend keep her job but Dante had laughed him off.

"She's not really in trouble although I fully intend to use this the next time I negotiate a scene with the little hellcat. She's been volunteering at the club in exchange for a radically reduced membership rate, so I'm going to enjoy this bit of leverage. She is hot as hell, and trust me when I tell you, this is no hardship."

Del had chuckled and known the man would only push the power he'd gained so far before backing off. No BDSM scene was worth a sexual harassment charge.

"Hey, really, man, don't worry about Suzy. She's a great employee, and it sounds like she gave you a glowing recommendation. She didn't tell Ms. Graham anything she couldn't have read in the gossip columns. She admitted to me she's seen you at the club but wisely kept that information to herself during her chat with Lilly Graham." *Wisely indeed.* Revealing any information about a club member would bring the fires of hell raining down on her.

"You two have the fucking luck, I'll say that for you. You're on a business trip halfway across the country and manage to get a date with a gorgeous woman who didn't run screaming from the restaurant when not one, but two strangers asked her out. She also happens to be neighbors and friends with one of my employees. Christ, man, go buy a fucking lottery ticket." Del could hear his friend chuckling as he disconnected the call.

Returning to the meeting after talking with Dante had been akin to the third level of hell. Listening as lawyers droned on about details no sane person gave a rat's ass about made him want to jump out of the twenty-second-story window. The conversation with Lilly had broken up the afternoon, but he still found himself glancing at his watch and wondering if the damned thing needed new batteries.

He'd made the arrangement for food to be delivered to her when he'd learned she was checking on them rather than enjoying her time at the spa. Dean had rolled his eyes when he'd learned Del planned to send a tray to Lilly's room. His brother reminded him many of the high-end spas were beginning to serve light snacks, but Del hadn't wanted to take the chance. Having it set up and ready to go with a simple fax had been a stroke of genius.

Letting out a sigh of relief when the meeting appeared to be breaking up, Del turned to his brother whose smile told him things had gone in their favor—no thanks to his own contributions. He was anxious to get back their hotel and get ready for their evening. When they finally stepped on to the elevator, Del was grateful none of the others lingering in the hallway had joined them.

"I'm convinced that was the longest meeting in the history of meetings." Del let his head fall back against the glass wall at the back of the elevator car, closing his eyes to block out his brother's knowing smirk.

"We've been in plenty of meetings longer than this one, but none of them sat between us and the lovely Lilly Graham." Del opened his eyes, leveling a look at his brother and was pleased to see nothing but genuine interest with a hefty sprinkling of lust.

"There is something about her, I don't know how to explain it. We locked eyes, and nothing could have dissuaded me from meeting her. I've never felt such a strong attraction to any woman. It was as if we already knew each other on some level." The only person Del had ever felt truly close to was his brother—he knew Dean almost as well as he knew himself. In many ways, he wished he was more like his easy-going sibling. As a Dom, Dean wasn't a stickler for protocol, but he wasn't a push-over either. Submissives who confused his easy-going manner with easy to manipulate, soon learned they'd made a serious mistake.

Most of their business contacts preferred dealing with Dean because he had a much more genial personality on the surface. What they didn't realize was it was a ruse— Dean was every bit as ruthless in business as Del, he just hid it better. His brother used the same people skills at the club and usually had a line of submissives seeking his attention, but he also took the term *play* seriously. For him, it was a way to find pleasure, but his pleasure wasn't tied to domination the way Del's was. Del often wondered if the right woman—the right submissive woman—wouldn't change the way his brother viewed the lifestyle.

"I had the hotel concierge send our suits out to be freshened and pressed. Did you make the arrangement for the car?" Dean's voice pulled him back just in time for the elevators gilded doors to slide open.

"Yes, I've ordered a limo because I don't want to limit our options." At Dean's raised brow Del shrugged. "I don't want to scare her away but holding back is going to be almost impossible."

"Don't get ahead of yourself. I agree, she is beautiful, but she's also building a modeling career. From what I can tell, she is making quite a name for herself. She probably travels more than not. That wouldn't be very conducive to what we're looking for in a woman. Hell, what am I saying? We're too young to settle down."

They opted to walk the short distance to their hotel since it would be considered just down the road a bit in Texas. Smiling to himself, Del doubted most New Yorkers would have found the mile and a half convenient or the stroll relaxing, but he had no interest in figuring out the complicated subway system. If he hadn't been distracted with thoughts of Lilly, Del would have been frustrated by the press of people all around him and the smell of garbage lining the streets awaiting one last pick up before nightfall. Nothing like the stench of ripped trash bags and the anticipation of seeing a beautiful woman to motivate a man to walk faster.

Chapter Three

L ILLY WOKE UP totally disoriented. She couldn't remember what day it was... hell, she couldn't even remember where she was. Damn, she hated coming off long road trips, the fatigue always turned her inside out in a hot minute before it knocked her on her ass.

Glancing at the bedside clock, it all came back in a flood of memories, and she jumped from the bed as if someone had set the damned thing on fire. Throwing off clothes as she went, Lilly was in and out of the shower in record time. By her calculation, she had less than a half hour before the West brothers were at her door... enough time if she didn't so much as take an extra breath.

As if she'd conjured an interruption, a loud knock rattled the heavy wooden door of her small suite just as she stepped out of the shower. Wrapping a towel around her, Lilly ran her fingers through her long hair in a desperate attempt to move it away from her face. Running through the suite, she was so harried she didn't even think before throwing the door wide open.

The look on Del West's face might have been amusing if she hadn't been so mortified. A part of her was grateful he and his brother were the ones standing on the other side while another much larger part was more embarrassed than she could ever remember being in her entire life. She wasn't usually so cavalier about safety... *I have got to get some damned sleep.*

"Shit." She dropped her gaze to the floor but not before she saw the heat in Del's eyes and the corners of Dean's mouth twitching with something that looked too much like amusement for her peace of mind. "I'm so sorry. I overslept. Could you come back in—"

"No." Del's one-word answer cut off her request for them to return after she'd gotten dressed. Without another word, the two of them moved forward to shield her from a rowdy group of young men making their way down the hall.

"Come." Once the boisterous trio had passed, Del wrapped his large hand around her wrist and pulled her behind him as he moved further into the suite. She heard the lock engage behind her and turned to see Dean following them into the living room. "Don't worry about him, Beautiful, he and I will always keep you safely between us."

EARLIER THAT AFTERNOON, Dean had watched his brother change before his eyes on the sidewalk outside a small café. He'd heard people talk about being love-struck, and Dean could safely say that's what had happened to his brother. One minute, they'd been discussing business as they walked to a meeting they been preparing for the past six months, and the next thing he knew, they were moving through a small but opulent eatery as Del zeroed in on the most beautiful woman Dean had ever laid eyes on.

Del had changed again when a breathless, wet, and nearly naked Lilly opened the door of her small suite. Dean's cock had swelled at the sight of her wrapped in nothing but a small towel, but Del's response had been completely different. Dean saw Del's entire body tense as he'd gone on instant alert, keenly aware of the three drunk men walking in their direction. There hadn't been time for them to get her inside and out of sight, so they'd done the next best thing and blocked her from the view of the guys who looked and sounded like they'd likely started partying mid-afternoon.

Once they were inside, an obviously flustered Lilly started to ask if they could return later, and she'd gotten her first glimpse of the dominant side of Del West. With one word, he'd silenced her, but it hadn't taken her long to regroup.

"No? *No?*" The incredulous tone of her voice was only topped by the increase in pitch. "You can't stay here while I get dressed. It isn't proper. I just got out of the shower. Can't you see I'm wet?"

Dean chuckled as he leaned casually against the door jamb of the suite's bedroom. He wouldn't stop her if she tried to make a break for it, but he would certainly slow down her retreat. She cast him a sideways look, and Dean saw the moment the double meaning of her words registered. Her face flushed a beautiful shade of pink, making him wonder if her ass cheeks would turn the same color under his hand. Her eyes dancing with fire, Lilly advanced on Del, and Dean waited for the fireworks to begin.

She managed to poke Del in the chest once before he shackled her wrist and spun her so quickly her wet hair flew in a wide circle fanning water droplets in a glistening arc that looked like floating diamonds before he pressed her firmly against his chest. Dean was near enough to see the flare of heat in her eyes as she found herself bound in Del's embrace.

Both West brothers had been raised on a sprawling

Texas ranch, but it had been Del who'd taken to binding a woman with rope. Personally, Dean preferred holding them with his words—the glazed look in her eyes after he'd taken her over the third and fourth time was what did it for him—but Del swore there was nothing sexier than a sub wearing the marks from his ropes.

DEL HAD BEEN shocked to his toes when Lilly opened the door covered in nothing but a towel he doubted was designed to wrap all the way around an adult. Her hair was still dripping, and she was clearly frazzled. Staring at them with a dazed look, her eyes impossibly wide, Del saw the moment she realized what a huge mistake she'd made a split second before mortification took its place.

She'd taken an enormous risk throwing the door open without checking to see who was on the other side of the door, but he'd seen relief when she'd realized it was them. That moment of reprieve was quickly followed by a flash of heat so searing, he'd wanted to pin her against the wall, seal his mouth over her pussy and watch as passion erupted in her beautiful blue eyes.

There hadn't been time to get inside and close the door before what looked like a trio of frat boys got to see more skin than Del suspected she would be comfortable showing them. *Who am I kidding? I was protecting the woman I've considered ours since the first moment I laid eyes on her.* He and Dean had stepped together in a perfectly choreographed move, forming a human wall to shield her from prying eyes. As soon as the rowdy drunks moved out of sight, they'd moved inside the room.

Knowing Lilly had heard rumors surrounding their

club membership and interest in ménage gave him the freedom to meet her request to return later head on. It didn't matter they were a few minutes early, there was no way he could walk away after seeing her in a way he was certain few men ever had. Their short interaction ended with her pressed against his erection and her easily misinterpreted comment about being wet.

"I suspect you are wet, and although I can't see the proof, I'm confident your sweet scent will drift up to me soon enough. Since we already know you are aware of our interest in kink, there doesn't seem to be any reason for you to play the *it's improper card*. Tell us, Beautiful, are you interested in the Dominant/submissive lifestyle?"

She went completely still in his arms, and he could feel her heartbeat pounding against the forearm he had pressed tightly under her breasts—breasts so close to popping free of their terrycloth confines, a deep breath was all it would take to expose her.

"Yes, but how?"

"How did we know you'd called a PI agency inquiring about us? Or how do we know what Suzy Quintara shared with you? Or perhaps you are curious how we know you and Suzy are friends and neighbors?" He nuzzled the soft skin behind her ear and was pleased to feel her shiver in his hold. Her confirmation and inquiry had been whispered so softly, Del would have missed it if he hadn't been holding her so close. Relief so great, it stole his breath for a few seconds moved over him. "I'll make you a deal. You get ready in half an hour while Dean and I enjoy a drink, and we'll tell you everything you want to know."

"Darlin', I'd take that deal if I were you because it's far better than the one I was going to offer." Del knew Dean was bluffing but also knew Lilly hadn't spent enough time with them to know Dean was usually the easier of them to deal with. Dean casting himself in the stricter role was total fiction.

Del felt the moment she resigned herself to them staying in the suite because she relaxed in his hold. He doubted she realized she'd arched her back, pushing the sweet curve of her ass tighter against his aching cock in an attempt to get closer.

"Thirty minutes is impossible." The airy sound of her voice made him long to hear how she'd sound shouting his name as she came around his cock. Her voice had deepened, and he smiled to himself when he realized her southern accent bubbled to the surface when she was aroused. Pushing his fantasy aside, for now, Del refocused his attention on the beautiful woman in his arms.

"No, it isn't, and the clock started when the offer was made. You're burning daylight, Beautiful." When she sighed, he opened his arms, releasing her. She walked the few steps to where Dean leaned against the frame, filling the door of her bedroom. His brother looked down at her, smiling and held out his hand. When she looked at him in confusion, Dean chuckled.

"Give me the towel, Lilly. You're a beautiful woman, it should be a criminal offense to hide all that loveliness under something so plain." When she looked like she was going to balk, Dean glanced nonchalantly at this watch— the not-so-subtle hint about her deadline hit its mark.

"What the hell, I'm about to fall out of the damned thing, anyway." Tossing it in Del's direction, she walked past Dean with her head held high, and it was their turn to blink in surprise. Holy fucking hell, the woman's body was a fucking work of art.

The door of the bathroom closed with a resounding

snick and Del let out a breath. "Christ in heaven, I need a drink." Turning to the suite's small bar, he poured bourbon into two different glasses dropped in a couple cubes of ice before handing one to Dean, then draining his in one large gulp.

"How many times have I told you, ice first, then booze?" Dean looked at the glass with a mixture of disgust and resignation. "You are such a fucking hick sometimes."

"You're welcome to pour your own damned drink." *Don't be such a pussy. Just drink it for fuck's sake. Del often wondered where his brother got his champagne tastes. While they certainly had the budget for sophistication, he'd never cared much for what his sweet granny had called 'putting on airs.'*

"Is that any way to treat the man who is responsible for your first glimpse at Lilly naked? Damn, she is full of fire and fucking gorgeous." Dean was right on both points, but admitting he owed his brother for demanding she hand over the towel wasn't an option. *No need to feed his already grossly over-inflated ego.*

"The body is fine, but the fire turns me on more than I can tell you." It was true, outside beauty had never been what drew him to a woman—it was why he'd never had a type. All the women he'd dated had one thing in common—they were always submissives. He couldn't imagine spending his life with a woman who wouldn't allow him to be in charge in the bedroom.

Del didn't mind sitting back and watching his brother work his magic with a woman every now and then, and Dean felt the same. They didn't share with anyone else, and until now, they'd enjoyed performing a few times a year, but Dean knew Del would never enjoy being on the club's small stage with Lilly. Hell, even he had to admit just the thought of a man other than his brother seeing her luscious bare ass and perfectly rounded breasts made the fringes of his vision turn pink as his temper flared.

"Don't get ahead of yourself, brother." Dean wanted his brother to reign it in, but the glare Del gave him didn't bode well for the conversation they needed to have. "Listen, I know she is amazing. Hell, she's even getting to me, but you need to stop and think about where she's headed in life and what we're looking for. I'm not sure those things are compatible in this case, no matter how much I wish it were so."

Del didn't respond, and Dean understood his brother was struggling to reconcile what he wanted with what appeared to be possible. Their future was tied up in the multi-national shipping conglomerate they'd been building for the better part of a decade. Thousands of people relied on them for their livelihoods, the vast majority of the men and women they employed Dean and Del knew by name. There was no way they could justify jeopardizing those men and women's futures or their families' safety and comfort. Could he accept having his scantily clad woman stared at by strangers? He wasn't sure… and he wasn't convinced his brother was level-headed enough to stand calmly by and watch men drool over her picture either.

Shaking his head, hoping to dislodge the image his thoughts provoked, Dean leaned his head back against the leather sofa and watched as his brother stared out the balcony doors. Knowing Del, he was wishing they were returning from the party rather than preparing to go.

Dean kept replaying the few seconds glimpse they'd gotten of Lilly bare as the day she was born. His cock protested being confined behind a steel zipper, and he had a feeling the situation wasn't going to improve much over the next few hours.

Chapter Four

LILLY MISSED DEL'S damned deadline, and so far, he'd stayed true to his word, refusing to answer any of her questions about how they'd known she'd talked to Suzy. When she'd threatened to call Suzy and ask, Dean had chuckled while assuring her Suzy was probably *tied up* at the moment. Del's snort let her know there was an inside joke, but they hadn't bothered to give her so much as a hint.

Sweet baby Jesus, it had taken her forever to regain her composure after her brassy move tossing the towel at Del and walking naked out of the room. What on Earth had she been thinking? She'd never done anything like that, and while it felt liberating, she also worried she'd given the West brothers the wrong impression.

She may have acted bold and confident, but the truth was, she rarely did anything spontaneous. Lilly's life had always been scheduled and planned to the nth degree. She'd rarely been given a moment alone, and her sister's penchant for getting into trouble meant their parents saw to it they were supervised by a staff who cared little about spontaneity and a lot about keeping their jobs.

There was something about Dean and Del... she didn't know how to describe it, but they made her feel safe, and that meant she could be brave and take chances. Dean's teasing manner challenged her to push herself, and she

30

suspected he'd be the one to encourage her to try new things. On the other hand, Del seemed like a man who would always catch you when you fell—an anchor during the storms of life.

They kept her between them during the limo ride, the warmth of their bodies flanking her own, making Lilly wish the drive had taken longer... a lot longer. Walking up the front steps of the Carlson's brownstone, Lilly wished for the hundredth time she'd listened to the devil on her shoulder who'd encouraged her to blow off the party and spend the evening getting to know the two men flanking her. She had a feeling things with Daisy weren't going to play out well and quite frankly, she didn't have the energy or desire to deal with a spoiled brat.

Dean's arm was wrapped casually around her back, pressing against her bare shoulder blade, while Del's hand was fanned over the sensitive curve just above her ass. Their touches were different, yet the same... the pressure just enough to reassure her they were still near. As soon as they'd stepped into the Carlson's foyer, Del guided her to the side, turning so he shielded her from the view of their hosts who were greeting other guests. The move was so protective, it reinforced her belief he would always be the rock-solid foundation in a woman's life.

Dean stepped forward to intercept Mary Beth whose face had brightened immediately when she'd seen them enter. Mary Beth Carlson looked a decade younger than any of her peers, making her one of the most envied yet least popular in her social circle. Women her age wanted to look like her, but most of those same women didn't want to be seen with Mary Beth because she unintentionally made everyone around her look dowdy. Lilly hoped she looked half as vibrant and beautiful as Mary Beth when she was her age.

"Are you all right, Beautiful?" The tenderness in Del's voice made the back of her eyes burn with emotion. "You've grown more and more tense since we left your hotel. If you are uncomfortable, we'll say hello to the Carlson's and beg off." Lilly was far more tempted than she should have been. She took a deep breath and hoped her forced smile would be enough to fool him... but one look at the frown lines between his brows told her it wasn't going to work.

"I'll be fine. This is not one of my favorite parts of my job. Even though Robert and Mary Beth are family friends... this is definitely a work event for me. I... well, I get tired of the pretense. It takes a lot of energy to feign interest in things you don't care at all about like social positions and kissing the right asses." He studied her for long seconds before raising a brow. She wasn't sure how he'd known there was more to her discomfort, but it was easy to see he wasn't going to be easily fooled.

"My sister and her friends will be here." When she nervously smoothed a nonexistent wrinkle from her dress, she could feel her fingers trembling as they brushed over her thigh. She'd hoped Del hadn't noticed, but it had been a pipe dream. When she met Dean's gaze from across the small room, he was frowning as his eyes zeroed in on her shaking digits. "Daisy is difficult on her best day but adding alcohol and an audience is a recipe for nasty on a whole new level." She paused hoping he'd take the hint and move on, but no such luck.

DEAN WAS RELIEVED when Del pulled Lilly to the side

because she'd been close to imploding. Since Dean had been playing the jovial lover role, Del stood a better chance of getting to the bottom of what was bothering her. He hadn't gotten the impression she was frightened, just far more stressed than he'd expected her to be. Hell, didn't models attend these parties all the time?

Intercepting Mary Beth Carlson before she could interrupt Del and Lilly's conversation, he'd been happy to engage the vivacious woman in conversation. They'd done business with her husband and quickly discovered what very few people knew—MaryBeth was the mastermind behind her husband's success. Whip-smart and stunningly beautiful, she and Robert had laughed after their first business meeting because neither he nor Del had treated her any differently than they had her husband.

"Most people underestimate my lovely wife based solely on her physical appearance. They assume she isn't bright because she is beautiful—it's the damnedest thing you've ever seen." Robert might have made light of the situation, but Dean had seen the frustration in his eyes. "She's brilliant, and I'd be lost without her." Robert had waited until Mary Beth was distracted by an assistant to lean closer.

"We've built a billion-dollar empire because I didn't let my pride get in the way. I was smart enough to use my greatest asset. I'm damned lucky as well because the woman who holds my heart in her hand loves me with a depth of passion most men can only dream of." Dean's respect for Robert Carlson had increased exponentially. In Dean's opinion, Robert underestimated his contribution to their success because the man could write an iron-clad contract God Himself probably couldn't squirm out of.

Mary Beth grinned as she tried to peek around Dean to

the shadowed corner where Del and Lilly stood. Dean knew his brother was keeping Lilly from view. He also knew Mary Beth was amused rather than annoyed one of her star guests was holed up just inside the front door rather than making small talk with the other guests.

"I hope Lilly is all right... I know parties are difficult for her." When he raised a brow in question, Mary Beth shook her head. "She doesn't model because she is enamored with it as a career. It pays great, and the money goes a long way toward paying for Daisy's education." Dean was stunned.

"Why is she paying for her sister's college education? We met Daisy earlier today, and she treated her sister deplorably." When Mary Beth frowned and nodded, Dean was even more frustrated. "You mean to tell me that's normal? She was rude, and it was obvious Lilly was embarrassed by her sister's behavior." Dean went on to explain how they'd met and was relieved to see nothing but affection in Mary Beth's eyes when she spoke about Lilly.

"I'm so glad she's met the two of you. It'll take two men to keep up with her. Once she gets to know you, Lilly is a firecracker." Dean wasn't surprised by the woman's assessment, but he knew the best way to find out more would be to stay quiet. "She's damned smart with killer instincts. She is also one of the most compassionate people I know, and truthfully, that's part of the problem... she doesn't stand up for herself."

Dean wondered if Mary Beth understood the power of her words. She'd just hit one of his hot buttons. If there was one tenant he believed in above all others in the lifestyle, it was empowerment. He wanted the submissives he played with to know themselves inside and out if for no other reason than the joy it gave him to see the newfound confidence shining in their eyes.

"If you don't mind me asking, why did you invite Daisy and her friends if you don't approve of the way she treats Lilly?" Dean was genuinely curious because Mary Beth didn't seem like the type who invited people to parties if there was a chance they would make others uncomfortable. He'd known hosts who delighted in inviting opposing parties, hoping the fireworks that were certain to follow would make their party the most talked about event of the year.

"Oh heavens, I didn't invite her, but she always manages to find someone to tag along with. I'd hoped she wasn't coming when I saw Lilly walk in with the two of you." As if their conversation had summoned the demon, Daisy and three other equally annoying young women walked through the door as if they owned the place, and Dean could have sworn he heard a very unladylike curse cross the lips of their ordinarily very gracious hostess. Chuckling, Dean leaned over to give Mary Beth a quick kiss on the cheek.

"If you need a couple of bouncers, please keep my brother and me in mind. It would be our great pleasure to escort her to the door." He heard her mutter something about holding him to it as he moved to where Del and Lilly stood.

Chapter Five

D EL WAS TORN between an overwhelming desire to protect Lilly and an almost equally strong urge to strangle her sister. Lilly had barely gotten the words out about her sister when Daisy's high-pitched voice filled the air. Jesus, Joseph, and Mary, her laugh sounded like the screeching witch in the elaborate Halloween display their mother had insisted on using for so many years despite their father's protests. She'd barely crossed the threshold, and she'd already managed to pull everyone's attention to her. Her voice reminded him of fingernails on a damned chalkboard and judging by the number of people he saw cringe, he wasn't the only one who thought so.

"Remember, Beautiful, all you need to do is say the word, and we'll have you out of here before you can blink." He didn't hold out much hope she'd take the out, but he wanted to put the offer out there... *again*. He watched as she took a deep breath and pasted on a smile so fake, he could only shake his head and laugh. Dean joined them a heartbeat before Daisy's ear-piercing squeal bounced off the walls of the large entry.

"Lilly. You're already here? You look... unusually plain, are you feeling all right?" Del felt Lilly stiffen as soon as her sister stepped through the door, but she'd gone positively rigid when her sister started speaking to her. He kept his hand pressed against her lower back, and Dean took her hand in his. Del watched his brother frown and wondered if Daisy had already pushed him over the edge or if something else bothered him.

"Thank you for your concern, sister dearest. Your *kind* assessment touched my heart and was just the boost my confidence needed. Thankfully, I'm fortunate to have dressed to impress my dates rather than my sister... and remarkably, they seem quite pleased." Lilly's saccharin smile and words were so phony, Del found himself smiling at how perfectly she'd painted her sister as the villain.

"Pleased would be an understatement, Darlin'. Del and I were speechless when we first saw you this evening."

Del struggled to hold back his laughter at the inside joke and the pink tint suddenly painting Lilly's cheeks. Amusement danced in her eyes, and he was pleased when he felt her relax against his hand.

"It's true. I'll never forget the vision she presented when she threw open the door." He might have been throwing gas on the fire, but Del couldn't help joining in on the fun. Robert and Mary Beth stepped closer, and the twinkle in their eyes spoke volumes. As Mary Beth led the women into their home's main room, Robert held them back.

"I'm not sure what that was about, but I smell an interesting story, and I'm looking forward to hearing all about it in the near future." The man they now considered a friend knew about their plan to share a wife and his open-minded acceptance had solidified their friendship. Robert and Mary Beth had a third in their relationship, but only a select few in their social circle knew about their kink. It wasn't the polyamorous relationship Del and Dean were looking for, but it was far more interesting than most of their staid friends' lives.

LILLY WAS GOING to strangle Daisy. She'd had enough of her sister's drunk and obnoxious behavior, and there wasn't any other reasonable solution. Now all they needed to do was figure out how to dispose of the body. Damn, they'd been at the party less than an hour, and Daisy's rabid behavior was completely over the top.

"I'm not sure what's going through your mind, Darlin', but it looks dangerous. You're not going to make us accessories to some heinous crime, are you? Because if you are, I'd just like to mention it's a lot easier to dispose of bodies in Texas." Dean's teasing tone made her smile, but it was a bit unnerving how well he'd read her.

"Well, I'm not sure I can wait three days. I don't suppose you have friends with a boat, do you? Wait, you own a shipping company, right?"

She hoped the smile she'd given him would be enough to distract him from the pain he'd see in her eyes if he looked closely, but she didn't hold out much hope for success. The best she could hope for was enough grace to have a few minutes to reclaim some of her dignity. Daisy's cutting remarks were meant to draw blood, and as much as Lilly tried to push them to the back of her mind, it still hurt. How could her only sibling be so callous?

Del was nearing the boiling point where Daisy was concerned... it was written all over his face, and Lilly hated knowing her sister would likely be the reason the West brothers walked away. Hell, it had happened so many times before, she'd lost track of the number of friends who'd slowly drifted away because Daisy was too much to bear. Del stepped in front of her, and when Lilly looked up into his dark eyes, she was surprised to see concern rather than annoyance.

"Tell me what you were just thinking, Beautiful. Don't edit and don't you dare lie to me." This was the second time Lilly knew she was seeing the Dom Suzy had alluded to—the tone of his voice brooked no argument, and she felt her entire body respond with a flash of heat that stole her breath.

"I was wondering if my sister's behavior was going to cost me two more *friends*. It certainly wouldn't be the first time. Most people decide she is too much and slowly disappear from my life. Honestly, I should just stop dealing with her, but…"

"But you pride yourself on keeping the peace, don't you, Darlin'?" Dean's assessment was dead on, and even though she knew it was impossible with Daisy, she still felt as though she needed to try.

"Are you ready to go, Beautiful? I'd like very much to get you away from your toxic sister, but before we go, I'd like to assure you nothing short of a nuclear blast is going to make us walk away from you. Quite frankly, I'm frustrated you would think we were that easily put off. Our interest in you has nothing to do with your sister, but I suspect time is the only thing that will convince you the wench doesn't have any real power in your life." She could tell he'd love to have labeled Daisy more accurately, but those southern manners were deeply ingrained. Del West wouldn't make a scene during the Carlson's party unless he was backed into a corner.

"You think Del won't deal with Daisy because he's reluctant to make a scene, don't you, Darlin'?" When Lilly turned to Dean, she knew he'd been able to see her surprise. That was twice he'd almost read her mind. "Don't look so shocked, your emotions are written so clearly in your eyes, it's almost like reading a book." His smile was a mixture of confidence and teasing, but there was a layer of steel beneath the surface Lilly suspected few people noticed. She understood all too well how easily people could be judged on outward appearances only.

"You're wrong you know." She must have looked confused as his words pulled her back from where she'd been lost for several long seconds. Grinning at her as if he'd known she'd taken a little mental road trip, he shook his head. "Del won't think twice about putting Daisy in her place, and he won't care who's listening. Neither of us will, Darlin'. We're tolerating her because you don't belong to us... *yet*."

"When you do, we'll deal with her." She was startled by Del's voice coming over her shoulder since she hadn't seen him move behind her. "No one will treat you as unforgivably as she has and walk away unscathed, Beautiful. We take care of what belongs to us." Del's words should have rankled her, but instead, they warmed a part of her that had been cold for a very long time.

In some ways, she'd always considered dealing with Daisy good training for the snobs she dealt with as a model. She'd been blessed with good looks and a great figure, but Lilly had always known the gifts had come from winning the genetic lottery, not from anything she'd done to earn them.

The fatigue of traveling and the mental exhaustion from dealing with her sister weighed on her until Lilly suddenly felt as if the world was fading around her. She was having trouble breathing and wanted nothing more than to get outside as quickly as possible. Trying desperately to pull back her growing panic, Lilly turned to the

French doors she knew opened into Mary Beth's lovely open-air atrium. It wouldn't be the same as being outside, but it was the next best thing, and right now, all she cared about was escaping the press of people all around her. She'd posed for a hundred pictures and signed everything party guests had thrust into her hands... and she was done.

DEAN WASN'T SURE what had gone through Lilly's mind, but the change in her demeanor had been startling. She'd gone from sad resignation to defeated exhaustion to utter panic in about two seconds flat. They needed to get her out of the crowd before any of the other guests noticed there was a problem. She didn't need someone leaking a story to the press about her having a meltdown in the middle of a party, and there was always the possibility some asshat would take pictures of her and sell them to the highest bidding tabloid. *I'm starting to think future generations will look back on our obsession with gossip as the beginning of the end of civilized society.*

Sheltering her between them, he and Del escorted Lilly through the atrium doors. As soon as they were inside the plant covered enclosure, Dean picked her up in his arms while Del stood blocking the view of anyone trying to see through the glass door. Moving to one of the benches hidden by the garden shrubs, Dean sat down with Lilly on his lap.

"Breathe with me, Darlin'. We're gonna do this nice and slow." He took a slow, deep breath and was pleased when she tried to match hers to his. Del stepped up behind her, and Dean was forced to make a fast grab to keep her from scrambling to her feet. Just as he'd suspected, she was worried about someone seeing her in such an unsettled state. Del quickly knelt in front of her and framed her delicate face with his large hands.

"Stay still, Beautiful, let Dean help you calm down, then we're going to go for that carriage ride."

Dean saw the relief in her eyes, and he nodded his head in the direction of the party after Del gave her a quick kiss.

"Mary Beth slipped her handbag in the drawer of the entry table. Make our regrets, and we'll meet you at the side entrance in a few minutes."

Del nodded before giving Lilly another quick kiss and making his way out of the atrium. It didn't take Dean long to calm Lilly once she realized they were leaving the party.

Rubbing circles over her lower back, Dean let the sound of a nearby water feature lull her into a calmer state of mind. He was amazed she'd unconsciously synched her breathing to his even after she'd calmed enough, he wasn't making her count the seconds of each breath. When she snuggled against him, Dean was happy to wrap his arms securely around her. Breathing in the floral scent surrounding them had been sweet but paled in comparison to the woman nestled in his lap.

"I'm sorry, I don't really know what happened."

Dean knew she wasn't being completely honest, but he suspected the deception was with herself more than with him. His priority was getting her settled and out of the Carlson's home without any further interactions with her damned sister.

"Can we go now? I need a change of scenery, and I'm looking forward to the carriage ride." He was glad to hear it but doubted she was as excited as he was.

"Up you go." Setting her on her feet, Dean stood beside her and smiled when she nervously smoothed the front of her dress. "Are you wearing panties, Lilly?" Her head jerked up, surprise reflecting in her bright blue eyes, but she didn't respond, so he repeated the question. "I asked you a question, Lilly, and I expect an answer... an honest answer. Are you wearing panties?"

He already knew the answer, but he wanted her to know Del wasn't the only one of them who was a Dom. Dean didn't live and breathe the lifestyle like Del, but he still enjoyed scenes with women he knew derived satisfaction from their submission. Despite her growing success, Lilly Graham was still a woman trying to find her way in a world where roles were changing so rapidly, most couldn't keep up.

"Of course, I'm wearing panties. It wouldn't have been proper to leave my pink bits out in the breeze... even if it might have been more comfortable than what I'm wearing." She probably hadn't intended to share quite so much information, but he'd learned a long time ago, patience was the name of the game when dealing with a woman who'd yet to discover the true depth of her submission. His silence had given him added information, and he intended to use it.

"Give them to me." The stunned look on her face would have been funny under different circumstances. "I've seen you naked, Darlin'. Handing over a pair of panties you've already admitted aren't comfortable shouldn't be a problem. My brother and I will want access to you during the carriage ride and panties are an unnecessary obstacle." Since the carriage driver was a close personal friend of theirs and a fellow Dom, she'd be lucky if they didn't fuck her senseless driving through Central Park.

Watching her eyes dilate until there was only a thin ring of blue showing made his already aching cock jump enthusiastically against his zipper but watching as her eyes flashed with fiery passion seared his brain. This was a woman who would challenge them in ways he suspected they had yet to imagine.

Without ever looking away from his eyes, Lilly reached up under her dress and slipped the small scrap of lace she'd been wearing down her legs. He pried his eyes from hers to take her small hand in his, steadying her as she stepped carefully from the tiny bit of nothing he could have easily shredded. One day soon, he'd take great pleasure in tearing an offending pair of panties from her and tossing it aside. When he saw her look to the side for a trash bin, he shook his head and held out his hand.

When she hesitated, he growled, and she quickly draped the delicate bit of lace over his palm. Lifting it, he pressed it against his nose and inhaled. Lilly's pink blush made him smile—despite being a well-traveled public figure, she'd maintained enough modesty to be embarrassed by an intimate gesture most experienced submissives claimed they found incredibly hot.

"As anxious as I am to smell her sweet scent, we have a problem to deal with first." Dean had seen Del re-enter the atrium but knew Lilly hadn't, so he wasn't surprised by her yelp of surprise when his voice sounded over her shoulder.

Chapter Six

D EL HAD BEEN seething when he'd first stepped back into the atrium, but watching his brother interact with Lilly had drained away enough of his anger, he'd finally been able to take a deep breath. He hated being the bearer of bad news, particularly when he had no idea how she was going to react, but it wouldn't be fair to wait.

"Your purse is missing, Beautiful. Mary Beth put it in a drawer in the front entry hall, but it's no longer there." Of all the reactions he might have expected, the rage flashing in her stormy blue eyes hadn't even made the list.

"I'm going to kick her ass. I'm not kidding, this is beyond the fucking pale. She doesn't care she's left me in the care of the two men she feigned concern about earlier today. Hell, she likened you to stalkers and the jerk I dated in high school. If she thought I was in danger, why would she ensure my dependence on you? It makes no sense... well, other than the fact she's a spoiled brat who cares little for anything or anyone who doesn't serve her purpose." Pacing the short distance between the shrubs surrounding them, Lilly's hands were flailing in the air, and Del was mesmerized by her.

"She takes the fucking fudge, you know that? She wanted my identification to get into a couple of the clubs she knows cater to the models at my agency. She'll act like a fool, and the owner will eventually figure it out, but I'll be left dealing with the carnage she leaves behind. I'll bet you rocks, marbles, or chalk, I know where she's headed. I'm going to catch a cab... fuck a fat fairy, she took my backup cab fare and my room key. I'm going to kick her inconsiderate ass, you just watch and see."

Dean was struggling to hold back a grin, and Del understood why his brother was amused with Lilly's tirade, but he needed to clear a few things up before they dealt with the situation with her sister.

"What do you mean back up cab fare?"

"I never like to carry credit cards or a lot of cash. It's just not really safe, you know? But if I go somewhere with someone else, I always take enough money to get back to my hotel as a safety precaution." She looked embarrassed, and she had no reason to be.

"That's a smart move, Beautiful. We're glad you take your safety seriously. If you belonged to us, we'd insist on it." She seemed to relax when she realized he wasn't angry. Pulling her into his embrace, he held her for several seconds before pressing a kiss against the top of her head.

"What club do you think your sister plans to gate-crash?" They didn't know every club in the city, but they knew several and were acquainted with the owners of the ones they frequented—perhaps they'd get lucky and have a contact who could help.

"She'll go to *The Destination* first, it's a favorite with her group of friends, but they can't usually get in unless I'm along. That is the real reason she was pissed I was attending the party with you instead of her... and as usual, Daisy has found a way to skirt the system. It's damned annoying, hell, she should have at least left my room key. I'll have to pay a replacement fee, and if she loses it, God only knows who might walk through the door." Del had the perfect solution, but he wasn't sure she was ready to hear it yet.

Dean had already moved to the side and was speaking on the phone. Del had been relieved when she'd named the club she felt Daisy would try first. They'd known the owner for a couple of years, and he was certain the man would be happy to secure Lilly's purse before he sent Daisy and crew packing.

"Come on, Beautiful. Let's get you settled in the carriage while Dean takes care of a little business." He chuckled at her delighted squeal when they stepped outside. Rather than admiring the vintage carriage, she'd hurried to fuss over Dolly. The enormous mare had been with Charlie for years, and both man and horse were beginning to slow down.

"Lilly, I'd like you to meet Charlie and his sweet girl, Dolly. Charlie... Dolly, this lovely lady is a fellow Texan." Charlie's face lit up with a huge smile as he shook Lilly's outstretched hand.

Charlie had been a family friend for as long as Del could remember. He sold his oil business after his beloved wife, Jean died a few years ago, and for much of the year, he traveled around the country with Dolly. Dolly had been Jean's horse for many years, and Charlie told him once, he wanted the sweet mare to bring the same joy to others she'd brought to his sweet Jean.

"It's great to meet you, Lilly. Dolly and I hail from eastern Texas ourselves. We travel around the country, and you caught us enjoying a bit of the city life before we start making our way back south. It's going to start getting colder soon, and these old bones don't move like they used to after Jack Frost makes an appearance."

"I'm thrilled to meet you and very much looking forward to having you show me the beauty of the city at night. I don't usually venture out after dark, so this will be a real treat."

Del found himself tuning out Lilly and Charlie's conversation as he focused on her body language. She'd relaxed as soon as they'd stepped outside and had become animated when he'd introduced her to Charlie and Dolly.

Seeing her long, slender fingers caressing Dolly's neck with a familiarity born of experience with animals squeezed his heart in ways he hadn't expected. Del watched Lilly rub Dolly's nose and couldn't help feeling a bit jealous of the horse's good fortune—he couldn't wait to have the sweet woman's hands on him. His cock was beginning to protest its confines in earnest, so he was relieved when Dean stepped up beside him.

"Holy fucking hell, I don't think I've ever been jealous of a horse before, but I want her hands petting me with the same affection she's showing Dolly." Dean's words echoed the thoughts that had floated through his own mind, but Del had the good sense to keep his envy to himself. Charlie was standing close enough to hear Dean's comments and didn't put much effort into hiding his amusement.

Del turned to Dean, quietly inquiring, "Did you speak with Brayden?" Brayden Hancock owned The Destination and its sister club, Chains which was housed next door. They'd been members of Chains since it opened several years earlier and had become friends with the owner not long after.

"Yes. He sent Marco to secure the purse and escort the women out of the club. They'll be banned for a year, and because Daisy was such a pain in the ass, they'll notify several other clubs as well. He's sending everything to our hotel via messenger—except Lilly's hotel room key and I.D. which were both missing. Marco didn't want to put his hands on Daisy to search her, and Brayden seemed pleased with his sub's loyalty." Del could only imagine the reward Brayden would come up with for Marco.

"Shit. It isn't safe for her to return to that room. Have you sent someone to clear it out and move her to our suite?" Del wasn't sure how she would feel about them taking over, but something about the missing key made the hair on the back of his neck stand on end.

"Brayden is sending a couple guys from his security team to take care of it. In case someone is waiting for her, we thought it best to send somebody who is packing." Shaking his head, Dean was clearly frustrated with the way things were playing out. "It's the nineteen-eighties, for God's sake, you'd think hotels would know better than to print their name on keys. When I called their security office, I was told they couldn't have the lock changed until sometime tomorrow, at the earliest."

"Why is it the fanciest places have the worst security? Hell, after Lennon, you'd think they would be damned careful with celebrities." Del was always stunned by the lack of security in New York hotels, especially those that were little more than insanely expensive apartment buildings. *I shudder to think what it's going to take to make this city sit up and take notice.*

The cooler night air gave them the perfect excuse to drape a blanket over Lilly's lap as they settled her between them in the carriage. They'd paid Charlie generously for a long ride since they knew all the proceeds went to various children's charities around the country. They'd also made sure something special would be waiting for Charlie when he returned to the stable where he kept Dolly while visiting the city. The two-hundred-dollar bottle of scotch should bring a smile to the elderly man's face.

As Dolly pulled them through the gate leading to Central Park, Dean smiled at the joy he saw in Lilly's wide eyes. Her enthusiasm was contagious, and Dean found himself looking around, trying to see things again for the first time.

DEL SLIPPED HIS hand beneath the blanket's edge and smiled at Lilly's startled gasp when he laid it over her knee. Pushing the tips of his fingers between her thighs as he slowly slid his hand closer to her uncovered pussy, he felt Lilly shudder and smiled down at her.

"Open those pretty thighs for me, Beautiful. I want to play with you while we enjoy our ride." The pink flush staining her cheeks gave her a look of innocence he hoped she never lost. "More. Remember, you've already admitted you're interested in the lifestyle, don't be afraid to go after what you want."

"We'll always catch you, Darlin'. There's no fear in taking a chance when you know we've got your back." Dean had done a great job of challenging Lilly, it was subtle, but Del saw the flash of fire in her eyes when the words registered. As a Texas native, implying fear was an insult—and to a Southern woman, it was one of the few words guaranteed to be met with an equal and opposite force. *Sir Isaac Newton has nothing on southern belles.*

Meeting the challenge head-on as he'd known she would, Lilly parted her thighs far enough he was able to press his palm against her slick sex. His cock responded to the heat, and her low moan stole his ability to think. Everything about Lilly Graham drove him to the very edge of sanity with desire, and suddenly, his sole reason for living was centered on giving her a mind-blowing orgasm.

Chapter Seven

ILLY'S MIND WAS racing, but it was rapidly losing ground to her hormones. She was reluctant to open her legs when Del first slipped his hand beneath the blanket, but Dean's challenge lit a fire deep in her soul she couldn't ignore. The minute his thick fingers touched her slick folds, her legs opened of their own volition. It didn't matter she'd known the West brothers such a short time, her body was so attuned to both men, it was humbling how easily they commanded her responses, often without saying a word.

She'd never responded to a man the way she did these two, and for the first time in her life, Lilly wondered if she could find the happiness she'd always worried would remain just out of her reach. Never having seen a successful relationship up close, it seemed like an impossible goal. Her parents only stayed together because neither of them was willing to forfeit half their assets or endure the drop in social status they knew would accompany losing half their friends.

"I don't know where your mind has wandered, Darlin', but you need to bring your lovely self back to us." Dean's warm breath moved over the sensitive spot behind her ear before he pressed a line of kisses down the side of her neck. When his mouth closed over the junction of her neck and shoulder, he bit down enough to make her suck in a quick breath. "There's a good girl. Focus on what you're feeling, the way our hands worship you with touch and let everything else go."

Del's devil-blessed fingers were sliding in and out of her soaking sex in a random pattern of strokes she found impossible to predict. The anticipation kept her on the cusp of the release her body craved but couldn't quite seem to grasp. Dean turned her slightly, so her back was cradled against his shoulder. The position further opened her sex to Del's talented fingers. When he rotated his wrist, curving his fingers, so they pressed against her G-spot, making her gasp, her body rocketed closer to release as it lit up from the inside.

She didn't understand why it wasn't enough to make her come, but the knowing glint in Del's eyes told her he understood perfectly. *If he knows, why isn't he helping?*

"Your body already recognizes its Masters, Beautiful. The release just out of your reach is waiting for our command." The pressure was building in her core to the point it was rapidly closing in on painful, and Lilly felt like her entire body might well implode.

"Please..." Lilly's brain was scrambling, the one-word plea all she could manage. She'd heard her friend Suzy talk about delaying orgasms, but Lilly hadn't thought the other woman was serious. When Lilly read the books Suzy loaned her, she'd been shocked to her toes because it was as if the author had crawled inside her head to take notes. Knowing others shared her needs had shaken Lilly more than she'd been willing to admit. The realization other people craved an escape from the pressures of everyday life wasn't hard to comprehend—what had blown her mind was all the ways a submissive could attain that escape.

Tears filled her eyes as desperate need clawed at her

insides. Between one second and the next, Del's eyes shifted from knowing indulgence to molten hot desire. He nodded to Dean, who turned her face to his, sealing his lips over her own.

"Come for us, Beautiful." Del's command was spoken with an air of authority her body recognized without any need for her head's involvement, and all the angels in heaven couldn't have held back the orgasm that stormed through her. Wave after wave of pleasure moved through her as brilliant fireworks lit up the darkness behind her eyelids. Seeing something so beautiful when she'd never experienced anything remotely this overwhelming was a welcome distraction from the emotional overload she'd been dealing with.

Sagging back against Dean, she felt tears burning the backs of her eyes. Not understanding the overpowering emotions rolling over her, all she wanted to do was curl up in the corner of the carriage and let her mind catch up with everything her body was feeling. When she looked into Del's eyes, she saw desire, but she also saw tenderness and understanding.

"Let Dean hold you, Beautiful, the crash is normal. Don't try to hide your feelings from us. When we say we want you, we want it all. We want to celebrate with you when you're happy, hold you when you're scared, and wipe away your tears when you are sad. Don't let the intensity of your response frighten you because it's something we'll always treasure."

Her head was finally beginning to clear, but she knew it was going to take her a while to fully process his words. When Lilly confessed her interest in the lifestyle to the West brothers, she hadn't expected... well, she wasn't sure exactly what she expected, but Lilly hadn't expected them to begin so soon. *Maybe it's one of those strike while the iron is hot, things?* They probably figured she'd back out if they gave her time to think about it. What they didn't know was she rarely backed away from anything she found frightening.

Modeling let her travel, but she rarely saw anything other than airports, hotels, and the locations where the shoots were scheduled. She made enough money modeling to pay for Daisy's college and incidentals—her parents had flat out refused to contribute any money to either of their daughters once they'd turned eighteen. It was getting harder and harder to keep up with Daisy's needs, and the one time Lilly suggested her sister get a part-time job to pay some of her own expenses, the ensuing drama had lasted for weeks.

Lilly was tired of handing over most of her earnings to a sister whose total lack of appreciation and respect had been taken to a whole new low this evening. She wondered if her newfound lack of tolerance was due to fatigue or the underlying knowledge Del and Dean would have her back if she finally took a stand against Daisy.

DEAN HELD LILLY close while she settled but noted there was an underlying tension that wasn't fading. He was certain her sister was at the root of the problem, but he didn't want to taint her afterglow by bringing up the woman who didn't deserve her sister's loyalty.

"Darlin', you have humbled us with the gift of your submission, and I assure you it's going to be even better when we get you naked and between us." He could almost feel her bringing herself back to the moment, and for just a moment, he wished they were already back at their hotel.

"We want you, Beautiful. As we've already said, we want all of you. I'm sure my brother will agree, the chemistry between the three of us is unlike anything we've ever experienced and far beyond what we ever imagined possible. We'd like to take you back to our hotel." Dean saw the hesitation in Del's eyes and knew his brother had already fallen in love with Lilly Graham. Hesitance and uncertainty weren't ordinarily in Del West's repertoire. "Even if you aren't interested in continuing to explore D/s, it isn't safe for you to return to your hotel."

Lilly looked between the two of them, and Dean wondered if she was searching their eyes for any hint of insincerity or if they were finally getting a glimpse of the sexy temptress he was certain lurked within. When a smile tipped up the corners of her kiss-swollen lips, he knew she was theirs—at least for tonight.

Dean saw Lilly's smile widen when she realized Charlie and Dolly had already stopped alongside the Towne Car the hotel had sent for them. Some of the tension drained from Del's shoulders when he saw Lilly's smile, but Dean suspected his brother wouldn't fully relax until they had Lilly naked between them. Since meeting Lilly, Del had uncharacteristically led with his heart, but it appeared his head wasn't going to relinquish all its power just yet.

As anxious as he was to get her upstairs, Dean was touched to see Lilly take time to say her goodbyes to Charlie and Dolly. Her pretty blue eyes went glassy with unshed tears when Charlie pressed his card into her palm along with instructions to call him if she ever needed anything. When Del began leading Lilly to the car, Charlie placed his arthritis ridden hand on Dean's forearm, bringing him to an abrupt stop.

"Take good care of her, Dean, she's very special. There is a fire that burns in her, but you'll need to fan the flames others have tried to extinguish. Don't be afraid of her career because it isn't feeding her soul the way making a life with you will." He was stunned by the older man's astute observation and even more interested in his comment about her career. "I want to be invited to the wedding, Dolly and I will be there with bells on."

In a flash of insight, Dean saw Lilly dressed in a beautiful white dress riding in a carriage as Charlie and Dolly brought her closer and closer to where he and his brother waited. The mental picture was gone almost before he was able to grasp it. Nodding his thanks to Charlie and giving Dolly's neck a quick hug, Dean made his way to the car with a renewed sense of what the future might hold.

Chapter Eight

LILLY TOOK A deep breath as she stepped over the threshold of the West brothers' suite. Something about the moment felt life-changing, but her thoughts were racing almost as fast as her heart, so she didn't have a prayer of sorting it out now. Taking in the massive open space before her, Lilly was amazed at the suite's old-world opulence.

The polished marble floors reflected soft white light from wall sconces she was certain had been converted from the original kerosene burners. The upholstered furnishings were new, but there were beautiful antique tables and lovely framed pictures from an elegant bygone era. She'd never seen such beautiful accommodations. The top tier models probably stayed in places this nice, but she wasn't ever going to achieve that level of fame... she didn't have the burning passion for it some of her peers did.

"This place is amazing. I've never seen a suite this lovely, and it's huge, how many bedrooms are there?" She didn't realize the implications of her question until she turned to face them and both men were smiling at her. She felt her face heat and knew she was blushing clear to the roots of her windblown hair. Her face had to be practically glowing from embarrassment.

"Beautiful, there are two bedrooms, and that's one more than we're going to need." Del's voice had deepened and sounded rough with what she hoped was desire. The books she'd borrowed from Suzy all mentioned the change in a Dominant's voice, but she hadn't understood how the shift could affect the submissives so strongly... until now. *My pussy understands even if my brain is slow on the uptake.*

"Listen to your body, Darlin'." She didn't know how Dean had known she was struggling with that exact issue, but his insightful words surprised her.

"That's right, Beautiful. Your body recognizes its Masters, but I'm going to disagree with you about your brain being slow. I think the opposite is far closer to the truth... your mind is working much too hard. We want to help you learn how to turn it off, so you get a much-needed break from all those pesky voices in your head. You're an amazing woman who has nothing to lose and everything to gain by giving herself to us."

Lilly took a couple of deep breaths to clear the panic starting to seep into her scattered thoughts. She wasn't afraid of Del or Dean, she was afraid of disappointing them.

DEL WATCHED LILLY'S expression shift and knew instinctively she was worrying she might somehow fail to live up to their expectations. He could assure her nothing could be farther from the truth but knew she wouldn't believe him. Only time would prove how safe she would always be with them. With every passing minute, Del became more and more determined to make Lilly theirs. He couldn't imagine leaving the city without her nestled safely between them.

Most people wouldn't understand how quickly Del had fallen in love, but he wasn't a fool, nor was he known for acting rashly. What Del was known for was making sound decisions and having killer instincts about people. Those instincts had never steered him wrong, and he was certain he was right about Lilly—she belonged to them.

"I'd like to tell you we'll take it slow, Beautiful, but I'm not going to make a promise I don't think I can keep. I want you so damned bad, I'm not sure I'll be able to make this first time as slow and romantic as you deserve, but I promise next time will be all hearts and flowers." Typically, it was Dean who was the more romantic of the two of them, but all bets were off with Lilly.

"Come." Del took her small hand in his, leading her down the wide hallway to the master suite. He wanted to smile when he heard her gasp. "It's lovely, isn't it? I think our guardian angels were looking out for us when we booked this suite. We've stayed in others at this hotel, but the clerk who checked us in insisted this one was perfect for this visit, and now I know why."

"Yes, we'll be leaving him a nice bonus when we check out." Del knew his brother was only half teasing. They had both been convinced the older clerk was out of his mind, but now Del wondered if perhaps he was psychic. Laughing to himself, Del refocused on the stunning woman standing in front of him.

Without giving her a chance to get any deeper in her own head, Del stepped forward to frame her face with his hands before lowering his lips to hers. The heat of the moment was searing and ramped up so fast, Dean had barely had time to unzip Lilly's dress before Del was scrambling out of his own shirt.

"I want you naked, Beautiful. My brother and I are going to explore every inch of you before we claim you as our own." He watched as Dean helped her out of her dress and was grateful Dean had already taken her panties. Without a bra beneath the beautiful halter dress, she was bare as soon as the slinky fabric pooled around her feet. "You are breathtaking." Using his fingertips, Del traced invisible lines down her toned arms and smiled when chill bumps followed his touch. Dean quickly stripped out of his clothing and moved behind Lilly.

"Spread your legs, Darlin', show Del what a pretty pussy you have." When she spread her feet less than shoulder width, Del knelt in front of her and moved her slender feet much farther apart. Using his knees to keep her legs spread, he heard Dean chuckle. "Oh, baby we're going to buy you a spreader bar to keep those pretty legs open for our pleasure. You've been spending too much time with uptight assholes who have brainwashed you into thinking ladies aren't ladies if their knees are apart, but I'm here to tell you, there isn't anything prettier than a juicy pussy swollen and ready for our attention.

Dean had given him the precious few minutes distraction he needed to pull himself back from his raging desire to fuck Lilly until they were both too tired to move. He wondered for the millionth time how men in traditional couples managed. It was a miracle mankind hadn't disappeared from the planet centuries earlier. *How they managed to romance a woman long enough to have children is a damned mystery to me.*

"When is the last time a man licked you until you came, Beautiful?" He knew his question surprised her, but he knew they were going to have to keep her out of her head and one of the best ways to do that was making certain she couldn't anticipate their every move. The only time he'd seen the light in her eyes dancing as her thoughts raced was when she was being totally bombarded by sensation. Earning her submission wasn't going to be easy, but it would be worth the effort, and once she learned how liberating it was to put herself in their hands, she'd give herself willingly.

"Never." Her confession had been laced with hesitant insecurity, and *that* was something he planned to erase quickly. From his position at her feet, Del could smell her essence, and his mouth watered in anticipation. Meeting his brother's eyes over her shoulder, Del saw the same determination in his expression. Her arousal fueled his own, and it was time to get this show on the road.

"I'm beginning to question the virility of the men you've spent time with, Beautiful." And wasn't that a damned understatement? How any man had resisted the urge to put his mouth on her perfect cunt was a mystery to him. Using the tip of his tongue, Del drew circles around her clit, trying to coax if fully out from under its hood. "Your clit is already coming out to play, sweetheart. It seems this little bundle of nerves is anxious for some attention."

"Attention we'll be happy to provide." Dean might claim he was only playing, but Del could hear the reverence in his brother's voice. Dean was every bit as enchanted with Lilly as Del was. Del knew himself well enough to admit he'd already fallen in love with her, and he was relieved Dean was falling in love with Lilly as well.

Del gave his brother a quick nod, indicating Dean needed to hold her tightly against his chest. He didn't want Lilly to fall if her knees folded out from under her, and given her sexual inexperience, it was entirely possible. She wasn't a trained submissive, and Del knew his brother was struggling to remember she wasn't one of the women he often played with at the club.

Leaning forward, Del flicked the tip of his tongue over

her clit and smiled when Lilly's entire body shuddered. It was going to be a joy to introduce her to all the ways he and Dean could bring her pleasure. Slipping his fingers through the slick folds of her pussy, Del relished the sweet honey flowing from her channel.

"So wet and ready for us. You please me more than I can say, Beautiful. We're going to make you come so many times, you'll forget your own name." *And you'll never want to leave us.* Del was already planning ways to convince her to stay with them in Texas. It would require more travel time for her, but he hoped he and Dean would be able to make it worth the sacrifice.

"I want to come. Please."

He loved hearing the sweet plea fall from her lips and couldn't wait to hear her screaming their names as she came around his tongue. Sealing his mouth over her clit, he sucked the sensitive tissues hard enough to make her tremble. He loved hearing her soft moans become gasps, and the sensations began washing over her like a tide crashing against the shore—each pulse of nature building upon the last until there was nothing left to hold back the surge.

Several more passes with his tongue, and he felt the telltale beginnings of her release. The muscles in her legs trembled against his arms, and she became so wet, the folds of her labia were becoming difficult to hold open. Pushing his middle finger in as deep as it would go, Del felt the muscles flutter around him.

"Holy handbells and Christmas carols. I'm going to come." Before she could draw in another breath, Del felt her fall over the edge. Her piercing scream would have probably brought security to their door if they hadn't accepted the upgrade to a penthouse suite. *Another reason the clerk is getting a nice bonus.*

Chapter Nine

L *A PETIT MORT.* Lilly was convinced the French had nailed it when they referred to an orgasm as *the little death.* She felt like she'd been blown apart, and she wasn't sure she'd ever be whole again. *Yeah, Humpty Dumpty has nothing on me.*

If she felt this fractured after oral sex and one finger pushing into her vagina, how was she ever going to survive them making love to her? Modeling might not be fulfilling her as much as she'd hoped it would but becoming a sex slave to a couple of millionaire playboys seemed like a rather extreme change of direction. *Just because it's extreme doesn't mean I'm not going to do it... just means I probably need to think about it for a while... say fifteen or twenty seconds.*

Every moment she spent with Del and Dean, Lilly felt herself falling deeper in love with them. The only part that didn't make sense was the ease with which it had happened. She didn't understand why it didn't seem strange to love two men when she didn't know anyone involved in a polyamorous relationship and had never even heard the term until she read about it in one of Suzy's books.

When she could finally manage to put her thoughts into words, Lilly looked between the two men and asked, "Have you always shared? Do you ever make love to a woman without your brother? Do you know anyone else who has a relationship like this one?" Del was studying her with an intensity she'd come to expect from him, but she'd also seen a flick of amusement before he schooled his expression. As expected, Dean didn't try to hide his amusement, his smile lighting up the moment and sending a wave of relief through her.

"Sorry, I know I can be a bit overwhelming at times. It seems once the questions start tumbling out, they all fall quickly."

"There's no reason to apologize, Beautiful. We welcome your questions."

"Even those we know you held back." She was surprised Dean had known she'd held back some of her most important questions. There was an underlying insecurity in her most people never noticed. Being beautiful was a mixed blessing. Beauty had opened a lot of doors for her, but it also meant most people never looked any further than what they could see.

After one serious dating situation turned sour, Lilly had never been brave enough to risk her heart again. That wasn't to say she didn't date, but she rarely saw the same man more than a few times, and with her current travel schedule, a long-term relationship would be nearly impossible, anyway. Firm fingers gripped her chin, turning her face to Del's.

"What put that forlorn look on your pretty face, Lilly? Remember, we want all of you—not just the bits and pieces you think we want to see."

What about those I'm afraid for you to see?

"I swear you might as well have spoken that question out loud, baby because it was written all over your face." When she turned wide eyes to Dean, he just chuckled. "You should never be afraid to be who you really are, Lilly. Whoever convinced you it was necessary to hide pieces of yourself didn't deserve the whole woman." His words warmed her heart, but it was his mischievous grin that made her wonder what he was up to. "Now, tell Del what he wants to know so we can fuck you, because baby, I'm telling you my cock is aching to be buried balls deep in your heat."

"I was thinking about how it would be virtually impossible to have a long-term relationship when my travel itinerary is so unpredictable. Modeling isn't the best job in the world, and it certainly isn't something I want to do long-term, but until Daisy is out of school, I'm stuck with it." It was the first time she'd admitted to anyone that modeling wasn't in her long-range plans, and it felt oddly liberating to speak the words aloud.

ON ONE HAND, Dean was thrilled Lilly trusted them enough to confess what he suspected she probably hadn't admitted to anyone, including herself. On the flip side, this wasn't the direction he'd hoped they'd be moving. Even though this was a conversation they needed to have, it wasn't going to get him inside her pussy. His cock was throbbing in protest, and it was taking more of his focus than he wanted to admit remembering strong relationships weren't built on sex alone.

The realization he wanted a *relationship* with Lilly shocked the hell out of him, stealing his breath and scrambling his senses for several long seconds. By the time Dean's brain kicked back into gear, Lilly was looking at him with something far too close to resignation for his comfort.

What did you expect? She's interpreted your silence as

agreement the three of you don't have any long-term future because she's sticking with a career she doesn't love to help a sister who doesn't deserve her devotion. I'd say that puts me damned close to the top of the asshat list.

"Beautiful, there are a number of very viable solutions, and my brother and I are looking forward to discussing them with you. We're not going to be easily dissuaded, I can assure you. You are everything we've been looking for, and we don't plan on letting you go." Dean watched as his brother easily soothed the tense muscles at the top of Lilly's shoulders with his simple words and a soothing caress.

The role of lover was usually Dean's, and he cursed himself for letting his damned brain get hijacked by his dick at a time when it had been critical for him to focus on Lilly rather than his own desires. As a result of his distraction, he now found himself sitting to the side, watching his brother romance the woman he knew in his heart belonged between them.

He'd never had any trouble staying in the moment when seducing a woman, but there was something so special about Lilly, he found himself in unfamiliar territory because, for once, *everything mattered*. Every word, every touch, every moment mattered, and it was unnerving as hell to realize how unprepared he was for this moment.

"Darlin' we might not always be able to travel with you, but there will also be many times when at least one of us would be able to go along." Her eyes widened as her mouth dropped open in surprise.

"I'd love having the company, but I'd be hesitant to take you away from business when the trips are so boring, I can barely tolerate the tedium. There wouldn't be any way I could, in good conscious, drag you away from your business when the shoots are always about waiting and more waiting. Do you know I've been to Paris three times in the past year, and I've never gotten to see any of the usual tourist attractions? I've only seen the Eiffel Tower from the small window of an airliner, and when I mentioned wanted to visit the Louvre, I swear to God, I thought my roommate's head was going to spin around on her head. My agent rolled his eyes until he could probably see his tiny little brain, and to be perfectly honest, I had a moment or two when I wondered what it would feel like to push him out the window."

Dean couldn't hold back his roar of laughter. Damn, the woman was an absolute delight. Life with her would always be interesting, and every minute they spent together solidified his desire for her. He wondered how quickly they were going to be able to convince her to marry them.

"Brother, I believe our corporate accountants may need to add a new line item for bail money. It seems our woman has a penchant for violence." Lilly's eyes widened in surprise at Del's observation, but Dean could see the sparkle of teasing in Del's eyes she hadn't yet learned to recognize. "Of course, I also believe it's because she has surrounded herself with people who deserve whatever she can throw at them, but that's not to say the local constable will feel the same."

Dean heard Lilly's small exhale of relief and wondered if she realized she'd barely been breathing, fearing Del's censure. Who had convinced such a remarkable woman she was anything less than perfect? Her open heart and giving nature were a large part of who she was, and obviously, those amazing traits had made her vulnerable as well. Dean and Del would take shielding her very seriously.

"We're going to talk about this... extensively... *later*.

Right now, I want you, and I'm tired of talking about obstacles I have no intention of letting stand in my way."

Dean wanted to laugh at Del's frustration. His brother was a businessman to the bone—solution oriented and results driven. Failure wasn't an option... ever. Hell, Dell had decided they would be millionaires by the time they were twenty-one before they'd even entered high school and had never so much as entertained the idea it wouldn't happen.

Between one breath and the next, Dean felt the energy in the room shift from casual conversation to flaming desire. The electricity crackling between the three of them was so powerful, he felt the hair on his arms standing up in response. Del took the lead, stepping close and pushing his fingers through the long strands of Lilly's hair to cup the back of her scalp with one hand and tracing the pad of his index finger over her lower lip with the other.

"We're going to show you what it's like to be loved by men whose sole purpose is to introduce you to the pleasures of ménage. Everything we do is with your pleasure in mind, Beautiful, don't forget that. You may not always understand the reasoning behind a command, and that's to be expected. What you do need to understand is everything is centered on you. There may be times when we'll fuck you for our pleasure, but tonight is about us showing you what it feels like to have two men focused solely on setting your sexual soul on fire."

"You're an amazing woman, Lilly, and it's going to take two men to keep up with you." Dean moved behind her and started smoothing his hands up and down her sides in agonizingly slow caresses meant to stoke the fire he knew Del was reigniting. "Two men so totally focused on you, they hear every sigh and feel every tremor. Their attention so centered on you, they can anticipate your needs before your mind can register them. Two men who don't miss even the smallest reaction because while one has his mouth fused to yours, plundering every recess with sensual sweeps of his tongue, the other is watching your sweet honey coat the petals of your sex in anticipation."

While he'd been speaking over her shoulder, Lilly had been so caught up in the words, she hadn't noticed they'd been slowly walking her back to the bed. Slipping his hand between her thighs, Dean moved his fingers through her wet folds and wanted to growl with satisfaction when he found her drenched with slick cream.

"You're so wet, Darlin'. We're going to reward you for that, baby." Pushing the tip of his finger into her heat, he withdrew some of her cream and used it to paint the outer ring of her anus, smiling when she groaned and pushed her sweet ass closer to his touch. "I'm going to love pushing myself deep into your ass, Darlin'. I'll go slow, so you don't feel anything but the sweetest kind of pain." By the time he pushed past the tight ring, she'd be so lost in the pleasure, the small bite of pain would be indistinguishable from the mind-bending pleasure.

Chapter Ten

D EL WAS CERTAIN his cock was going to burst, it was so hard. The blood pounded inside him, making the skin covering his penis so sensitive, the brush of air as Dean lifted Lilly, so she straddled him threatened his control. The heat from her pussy enveloped his cock, and for the first time since he was a teenager, Del thought he might actually come before he was fully seated in the woman he was making love to.

Mentally reviewing the details of their latest contract negotiation, Del tried to force his body to hold back the urge to plunder and claim. The caveman inside him was clamoring to the surface with remarkable speed, and Del took several steadying breaths to bring himself back under control.

"You test me in ways no other woman ever has, Beautiful. I'm going to let you push yourself down on my cock because I don't want to risk going too fast and overstretching those sensitive tissues." He gave her a wicked smile and was relieved to see her take a deep breath. "Remember this moment because I won't often let you be in control. The only stipulation is once you begin, you must continue making steady progress until you've taken every inch. Don't stop and don't withdraw unless you've used your safe word." Since she'd already confessed to reading about the lifestyle, he knew she'd understand.

"Later we'll have a nice chat about protocol, but for now, I want to remind you that you can use the word red and everything stops. But you're only to use it if you are so overwhelmed, either physically or mentally, you simply cannot continue. If you are beginning to feel fearful or need to slow things down, use the word yellow, and we'll stop and talk."

Del wanted to roll his eyes at Dean's rule review. It didn't matter he understood the necessity, all he could think about was how it was going to feel as she pushed herself down over his cock.

When the sensitive tip of his cock head moved slowly to her opening, Del heard himself groan. The heat was exquisite, and he hadn't even begun pushing between her flexing vaginal walls.

"Fuck, she is already rippling around me, and I'm not even all the way inside yet. Beautiful, you can come as often as you like. Don't hold back unless we tell you to."

Every release would relax her even more, making it easier for the two of them to take her together. Her petite frame and inexperience meant this first time was going to be an exercise in restraint. Del sent up a silent prayer of thanks for Dean's expertise in anal sex. His brother knew more about the nerves and muscles of a woman's ass than any Dom Del knew. He'd studied every aspect of ass play and knew how to ignite a firestorm and coax a woman's body into relishing the heat.

Lilly grasped his shaft in her small hand, and Del felt his cock jerk in response to the warmth of her gentle touch. Later, he'd show her exactly how firmly he liked to be handled, but for now, it was taking all his focus to keep from flexing his hips and pushing in as far as he could in one fast, hard move. She guided his tip deeper into her opening and heat enveloped him in a rush.

"Jesus, Joseph, and sweet Mother Mary. Your pussy is an inferno burning me alive, and we've only just begun, Beautiful. Take it as slow as you need to, but don't stop moving now that you've started." She pushed slowly down over him, and he smiled when her head fell back, sending the soft waves of her chestnut colored hair down to brush over his thighs.

"You're so big, so hot. The stretch is burning me up, but it's so good... so damned good I'm going to c—" she didn't finish before he saw her stiffen.

Her tight vaginal walls clamped around him with surprising strength, and he felt a fresh rush of cream wash over his cock. Watching as a small orgasm swamped her, Del was beyond pleased she'd responded so perfectly. When she started to lift herself from him, she realized he was still hard inside her, and her eyes widened in surprise before a shadow of disappointment moved over her entire expression.

"You didn't... well, I mean you're still hard." The sheen of tears in her eyes surprised him.

Did she think he hadn't enjoyed himself since he hadn't come at the first opportunity? What the hell kind of pansy-ass men has she been with?

"Oh, I assure you, I enjoyed myself immensely. I was worried I was going to lose my mind from the blinding pleasure, but we're not nearly finished with you yet, sweetheart. We'll always strive to make certain you come at least twice before we do." Her eyes widened in surprise before a slow, sexy smile curved her kiss-swollen lips.

"I'm not sure I'll be able to survive the two of you, but I'm going to enjoy the ride." He heard her unspoken acknowledgment their relationship wasn't going to last, but he let it pass. It was time to claim her—and once they'd given her a glimpse of the pleasure of ménage, he hoped she'd see there were other advantages of a polyamorous relationship as well.

DEAN WAS CONVINCED his entire body was going to explode into a steamy mist if he didn't get inside Lilly. He knew Del wanted to get her closer to an emotional center before they continued, but Dean didn't want to give her a chance to worry about what was to come. Pressing his hand between her shoulders, he moved her lower until she was pressed against Del's chest.

Watching his brother wrap his arms tightly around her upper body, holding her firmly against his chest as he whispered soothing words of encouragement, Dean grabbed the small bottle of lube he'd set nearby. Drizzling the cool liquid at the top of her crack, he let it slither over her puckered opening and smiled to himself when she gasped in surprise.

Don't worry, Darlin', we're going to go so slow, you'll be begging me to take you before I'm done." He knew it was true, but he doubted she believed him—yet. Taking his time, he carefully massaged the outer ring of muscles, rimming her anus until he saw her arching and lifting into his touch. "Perfect. Watching you press closer to the pleasure of my touch turns me on in a way I don't even know how to describe.

"Please. More." Her voice was light and airy but also laced with a need he planned to sate in a way they would all enjoy. "It's so naughty. So perfectly decadent, and I want it more than my next breath." She might think she was ready, but he and Del had experience on their side, and they still had a long way to go before she'd be stretched far enough to take them at the same time.

"Beautiful, let Dean prepare you properly, so you don't feel any more pain than is absolutely necessary. We aren't sadists, so we haven't spent a lot of time studying pain. We prefer playing on the edge where a small bite of pain falls in the blurry nether-world where pleasure and pain are indistinguishable." When Lilly didn't respond, Dean leaned forward gently biting down on the sensitive place where her shoulder curved into her slender neck. He didn't bite hard enough to break the skin, but it was firm enough Dean knew she would carry the mark for several hours.

"Tell, me Darlin', was that pain or pleasure?" He'd already breached her rear hole with the tip of his finger and was fucking her slowly, pushing deeper with each pass, so he knew she was being bombarded with sensations that would be difficult to distinguish one from the other.

"Two... oh, God, it's two sides of the same coin just like the book said it would be. Both. It hurts so good, there are fireworks exploding under my skin, lighting everything up from the inside out."

"Fucking hell, she is already clamping down on me, and I'm not sure I'll be able to hold out against another storm." Dean didn't remember ever hearing Del sound so desperate.

He'd finally stretched her to three fingers, so she was a ready as he could make her. Donning a condom he'd set out, Dean generously lubed his aching cock and pressed the tip against her opening.

"Push out with your muscles, Darlin'. That's it." She was a natural, hell, she'd been pressing back before he'd finished speaking. "You're so fucking perfect. The heat alone is tipping me close to the damned edge." Dean heard Del remind her to breathe, and for the first time in his life, Dean realized he'd needed the reminder as well.

Sucking in a deep breath, Dean was grateful she hadn't been able to see his control slip, but his brother hadn't missed it. Del gave him a knowing look over her shoulder, and for the first time in years, Dean heard his brother's thoughts echo in his head as clearly as if they'd been his own.

I know... Nothing in the world could have prepared us for her. She is a Texas tornado, a tropical hurricane, and a bolt of lightning, all rolled into one delicious package.

Dean heard her whine as he pushed past the tight ring and realized his brow was sweat-drenched as he worked to hold back. The urge to thrust forward and sink deep was almost more than he could take.

Inching in, bit by bit with small thrusts and retreats, Dean could hear Lilly's low moans as she lost herself in the pleasure. She was trembling in Del's arms, and he knew she was ready for more by the way she was pushing back. Giving his brother a nod, they began alternating their strokes, so one of them always remained buried inside her.

"Oh, God! It's so good... like flying without ever leaving the ground." Lilly's voice was strained, but he was thrilled to know what she was thinking since he couldn't look into her eyes.

Del had loosened his hold on her enough to be able to see her face, and the love Dean saw in his brother's eye spoke volumes. *I'm not sure I've heard anyone describe it any better.*

"Come for us, Love, and take us with you." Del's words must have broken the silent hold she seemed to have on her release. Dean felt her body begin to shake, and when she screamed their names, he and Dell both followed her over. Light exploded behind his eyelids, and for several long, shuddering seconds, Dean wasn't sure his arms were going to support him.

"As soon as I regain feeling in my arms and legs, I'll move, but until then I'm content to feel all those sweet aftershocks rippling around me." Sucking in a deep breath, Dean leaned forward just enough to press a kiss between Lilly's sweat-covered shoulder blades. Everything inside him had fallen into alignment the minute they claimed her as their own. Sharing her body was only the first step, but it had been a huge one. Lilly hadn't hesitated to make love with them both at the same time—hell, she'd taken to a full ménage as if she'd been made for it.

Lilly lay draped over Del like an exhausted rag doll. She was no longer gasping for breath, but she wasn't moving either. Del had a dazed look in his eyes Dean had never seen before, and he suddenly realized how different things were when it was the woman you intended to keep.

"You killed me. Death by orgasm. I'll come back to haunt you—hide your keys, move things around, make your fire alarms sound for no particular reason during business meetings. All the usual cheap poltergeist tricks."

Del's rumbling laughter made Dean smile. There would never be a dull moment with this woman in their lives.

Twenty minutes later, they'd all showered and were walking back into the bedroom when Lilly tripped falling into his side. Dean wrapped his arms around her and easily lifted her into his arms.

"We're sorry, Darlin'. It seems my brother and I haven't taken into account how tired you must be after traveling for so many weeks." Del had the bedding turned down, and Dean set her as close the center of the enormous bed as he could.

Dean turned out the lights, slid into the bed, and sealed his lips over hers. He'd planned to give her a quick kiss goodnight, but when she opened to him, all bets were off. Pushing his tongue between her lips, tasting the sweet woman who'd given herself so selflessly to them sparked a fire inside him, but this one was in his heart rather than his groin.

"You need to rest, Beautiful." Del's voice over her shoulder pulled Dean back from the edge, and he nodded to the man he'd often considered the other half of his soul. Now that they'd found Lilly, Dean was going to revise his observation—they were each one-third of a whole.

Chapter Eleven

D EL AND DEAN were escorting Lilly to an appointment
the next day when they met a business contact and
paused on the sidewalk to greet him. Lilly smiled and
shook hands, but then pointed to a small coffee shop across
the street. Del pulled her into his arms, telling her they'd
join her in just a moment before releasing her and turning
his attention back to Christopher Tallon.

Chris mentioned a project he was working on, but before either Del or Dean could respond, the sound of tires
squealing and people shouting drew their attention.
Looking toward the street where Lilly planned to cross,
Del felt his blood turn to ice as the scene played out in
what seemed like the slow motion reserved for horrifying
events.

A large black SUV was turning left despite a red light,
and Del saw Lilly standing in the street. He and Dean both
took off running, but they didn't have a prayer of reaching
her in time. He had only taken a few steps when heard her
scream a split second before the sound of her being hit and
then bouncing off the hood filled the air. She rolled to the
far side of the vehicle just as the driver accelerated and
disappeared down the street. He was only able to get the
first portion of the license plate numbers before it was
gone.

Del was astounded to see people walk around Lilly's

crumpled form lying in the middle of the street as if a battered woman bleeding on the asphalt was an everyday occurrence. *What the hell has happened to this country that made people value their time more than they did someone in need of assistance? When did we stop caring?* Pushing away those thoughts, Del was relieved to see a young couple run up beside them as he and Dean knelt beside their lifeless beauty.

"Fuck, she is so damned still. Is she even breathing?" The woman who'd approached leaned forward and nodded.

"Make sure someone has called EMS, then tell me everything you can, no matter how insignificant you might think it is." Del stared down at the woman who appeared to be examining Lilly, but he was too stunned to respond.

"My wife is a physician, and I'm a detective. We'd like to help, but we're going to need your cooperation."

Dean was brushing Lilly's hair away from her face and murmuring quiet words of encouragement, so Del moved a few steps to the side and told the detective what little he knew. Del studied the detective closely, there was something familiar about the man jotting notes, but Del couldn't place him. When Del gave him the tag information, the detective pulled his phone from his pocket and passed along the information Del had given him.

Another woman standing nearby assured the doctor she'd already called 911, and Del felt his heart thaw at the acts of kindness taking place around him. Several men in suits were directing traffic around them, so Lilly didn't have to be moved. Even to Del's untrained eye, it was obvious she'd suffered a broken ankle, and the sickening angle of her arm indicated it was broken as well.

"Her pulse is strong and steady, pupils reactive, but her

respiration appears labored, so we'll need to check her for broken ribs, but the change in breathing is often simply a reaction to the trauma. She's starting to rouse, so we need to keep her as still as possible." When it became obvious she wasn't responding to Dean's attempts to keep her from thrashing about, Del moved closer.

"Stop! You are to lie still and let the doctor finish her examination, Beautiful. Do not move unless you are directed to do so." He was pleased when she immediately stilled, and her eyes slowly fluttered open. When Lilly blinked several times, trying to focus on his face, Del felt his heart clench as he smiled down at her. "Good girl." When the doctor looked up at him with knowing eyes, Del raised a brow at her in question.

"I doubt you remember me, Mr. West, but we were introduced by Brayden Hancock a couple of years ago. My husband and I had recently joined his club, and you were in town for a meeting." Del studied her features for a hint of recognition, but nothing jogged his memory until she commented on what she'd been wearing.

Her Dom had carefully removed the lining from a lace dress before giving it to her for a kinky formal night at the club. As a newbie, she'd been mortified by having what she'd referred to as her girly parts put on display—a complaint the small group of Doms in their group had quickly dismissed, considering her occupation. Smiling at her pink cheeks, Del nodded.

"I'm sorry, I'm usually better with faces. I think per-haps seeing my lovely woman tossed in the air by a speeding car has scrambled my thoughts a bit." The glare of flashing lights and din of approaching sirens cut off their communication as they were quickly surrounded by emergency responders.

"No problem, I understand. Being out of control isn't most Doms strong point. It was a lovely dress, and I'm not nearly as shy as I was.

"I was on my way to the hospital, so I'm going to ride in the ambulance with her. When you get to E.R., check in with the head nurse, and she'll bring you back as soon as she can."

The sparkle in her eyes put him at ease, and he appreciated her making the effort to keep her comments private. It was a relief to know a member of the kink community would be looking after Lilly.

The last thing Del heard and the doors on the back of the ambulance closed was, "My arm hurts like a bitch, but I want to hear about your dress."

THE FIFTH TIME Dean's phone vibrated in his pocket in less than five minutes, he reluctantly pulled it free and wondered what on earth Dante Radison needed so badly, he was calling continuously. Answering as the taxi they'd hailed drove like it was trying out for a place on the Nascar® circuit, Dean hoped like hell he'd be able to carry on a conversation with his life hanging by a fucking thread. The driver cursed in a foreign language Dean didn't recognize as they squeezed between two other cars, and the sound of scraping metal filled the cab, making Dean revise his opinion—their driver had obviously been a demolition derby driver in his first life.

"Damn, West, what the hell took you so long to answer?"

"Well, we've had a bit of a *situation* here." Dean couldn't imagine what on Earth had Dante's tighty-whities in such a twist, it was completely out of character for the Dom known for his control to be so rattled.

"I'm afraid things are going to get worse. There's a contract out on your woman." Dean was too speechless to respond. Dante obviously mistook his shock as waiting for additional information and rattled on. "It seems she's angered one of the local drug lords by fucking his son in the back room of a local club, then walking out with a roll of cash the young man had been flashing around earlier in the evening." *What the fuck?* "Whoever this was, conveniently left an identification card with Lilly's name on it and hotel key on a small table."

Finally finding his voice, Dean asked when the incident took place and wasn't surprised to learn it had been last night. Her fucking sister had not only pulled a seriously dangerous boner, she'd thrown her innocent sister under the bus—or SUV as it had turned out. His mind was finally jolted into gear as he slammed into the side of the taxi when it rounded a corner on two wheels. The damned driver had taken Del's promise of a huge bonus all too seriously. Hell, they were liable to be patients by the time they reached their destination.

"You're in fucking Dallas, how is it you heard about this before we did?" To be honest, Dean wasn't even sure why he'd asked. He'd learned a long time ago to not question how Dante found shit out, the explanations were often scarier than his imagination.

"When I learned you were interested in her, I set her up in my system. I didn't give up two rooms of this place for that damned computer for no reason. I swear the lights up and down Commerce Street dim when I fire that bad boy up every morning." When Dante chuckled, Dean knew he'd been had. "Nah. I've got friends and word travels fast." Dean wasn't going to push because he knew Dante would continue dancing around the answer. He just wished he'd gotten the information an hour ago.

"Thanks for the heads up, man. I'd say this means the damned SUV that hit Lilly, and then took off like a scalded cat was more than some careless asshole who didn't want to fill out a bunch of paperwork." Even as he spoke the words, their truth hung heavily in the air.

He finished his call as they pulled up near the emergency entrance of the nearby hospital. Del paid the driver what looked like a fistful of hundreds, and the grateful man handed him a card with a hastily scribbled phone number on the back. *Like I'm ever getting in a car with you again, Mario.* Hell, Andretti had nothing on this joker.

Dean was already speaking with the head nurse in the emergency department by the time Del finished paying the cabbie and made his way inside. Trying unsuccessfully to charm the forty-plus-year-old nurse who had probably already heard every conceivable lie, Dean sagged when nothing in his arsenal worked.

Del shook his head in disgust and held up a card for the nurse to see. "Dr. Breck said she wanted to be notified immediately when we arrived. The woman she accompanied here is my fiancé." *Fiancé?* He wasn't sure if his brother was lying or simply guilty of wishful thinking. *Maybe he's psychic? That works for me.*

Dean schooled his expression as the battle ax studied their expressions closely, no doubt looking for any hint of deceit. She could give it up—he and Del hadn't built a multimillion-dollar business wearing their emotions on their sleeve. Hell, their mama had always sworn Del could lie to God, and even though the nurse appeared to be immune to his charm, she was responding to Del's air of authority.

The nurse reluctantly turned to one of her underlings, sending the younger woman scampering down the hall in search of Dr. Breck. When she returned less than a minute later, she confirmed they were supposed to join Lilly as soon as they arrived. With a disapproving scowl, she directed the younger woman to escort them to the back.

"Your fiancé was only given a small dose of pain medication, so she can be closely monitored for concussion symptoms. She seems to be a bit sensitive to the medication so you may notice she isn't acting quite herself." Dean wanted to roll his eyes at the blatantly understated comment. *Damn, I can understand covering your ass, but this is over the fucking top.*

They rounded another corner, and the sweet sound of Lilly's voice greeted them.

"Where are Del and Dean? I thought you 'all said they were just down the hall. They are both tall fellas so their long legs will eat of the distance in no time flat."

Dean had to fight the laughter he could feel threatening to break free. Part of it was amusement at her words and the deepening of her accent, but a larger part was the sheer relief knowing she was okay. Damn, they'd come much too close to losing her for his peace of mind. Grasping his brother's elbow before they stepped into the room, Dean met Del's questioning gaze.

"We have to get her back home as soon as possible. It's not safe for her here. And if I'm forced to deal face to face with her damned sister, I'm not going to be responsible for my actions."

"Agreed. I've already put the pilots and crew on standby. Robert and Mary Beth are getting everything from our room moved to the jet. I didn't want to risk her returning to our hotel. Brayden is looking for Daisy and will put her ass on a commercial flight as soon as he finds her." Del scrubbed his hand over his face, a gesture Dean recognized too well. His brother was getting ready to suggest something he didn't expect Dean to go for.

"Just spit it out before they send out a search party for us." Lilly was currently gasping in horror at the color selection for her casts. It was time to distract her and save the medical staff some serious aggravation.

"I want to pay off Daisy's education and take the burden from Lilly's shoulders." Dean knew there was more to it, so he simply waited. "I want to strip the venomous witch of any reason to contact Lilly in the future." And there it was—the heart and controlling soul of Del West.

"I agree, you can set it up, but the final decision isn't yours to make, brother. For what it's worth, I agree, but we'll lose Lilly if we try to force our will on her about this. Trust her to make the right decision. As long as we don't lose Lilly, we'll be able to minimize Daisy's influence." For the first time in too many years to count, Dean saw uncertainty in his brother's eyes.

They'd spent their entire lives pushing to reach this point in both their personal and business lives, and he'd never seen Del waver. They were both goal-oriented to the max, but their approaches to problems were often vastly different. Before the discussion could get any deeper, they were interrupted by Lilly's ear-piercing scream.

Chapter Twelve

"YOU CAN'T GIVE me pink and blue casts. What in God's holy name is wrong with you? Do I look pregnant to you? Boy, oh boy. You're going to ruin everything. Del and Dean are going to take one look at me and decide I'm not worth the trouble, and it's all going to be your fault. Well, you and Snidely Whiplash, since he was driving the car."

Del had been amused by the casts comment, stunned by her suggestion they'd walk away because she'd been hurt, and made a mental note to pass along the cartoon description of the driver to Detective Breck.

"Beautiful, we're going to have a long chat about your mistaken impression we're letting you go for any reason." Del was glad he'd already started speaking before he entered the room because seeing the scrapes and dark bruising he knew was only going to get much worse would have stolen his words. Her left cheek looked like someone had pulled her facedown behind their truck along a sanded road. There were still tangles in her long hair, but it did look like someone had made at least a half-hearted effort to clean the dirt and small pebbles he knew had been there earlier.

"Darlin' you'd have to try a lot harder than this to get rid of us." Dean moved around where Del stood rooted in place to stand in front of Lilly. Leaning close, his brother pressed a gentle kiss to her forehead and shook his head. "Sweetheart, you're a mess, but as soon as we can, we're going to whisk you right out the door so we can spoil you rotten." The glassy tears that filled her eyes before spilling over to stream unchecked down her cheeks were all it took to uproot Del's feet from the floor.

"Dean is right, you're ours, and until this is resolved, we're not letting you out of our sight, Beautiful." The glazed eyes from the pain meds told him she wasn't functioning anywhere near one hundred percent, so he didn't want to go into any of the details of what they'd learned about the incident or Daisy's part in it.

The doctor finished the cast on her leg and looked up grinning. Del felt his heart warm when he recognized Dr. Cal Martin. The man nodded to them and chuckled when Lilly started singing *Lovers Live Longer*, doing a fine rendition of the Bellamy Brothers hit until the nurse urged her to hold it down. They'd gone to school with Cal in Texas but lost contact once he'd gone on to medical school.

"Holy shit. You're the hotshot orthopedist Brayden was calling in?" Del felt himself beginning to relax for the first time since he'd watched Lilly sail through the air.

"I'd already called Cal before Master Brayden had a chance." Del raised a brow in question when Dr. Breck referred to the club owner as Master rather than Mr. She blushed, and Cal chuckled.

"It's okay, Lynn, these men are experienced Dominants, you won't shock them."

Del laughed because they hadn't seen Cal in several years, but distance wasn't a huge factor in the kink community—word still traveled fast. "Lynn, Dennis, and I have a polyamorous relationship, much like the one I suspect you are planning to build with our lovely patient."

"Aww, isn't he a sweetie, calling me lovely when I probably look like I got run over by a truck? Wait. I did get run over by a truck, didn't I? Why did Snidely run over me? He tried, you know… I saw the look on his face. He aimed right for me. Why would he do that? Hey, I don't want you to put that on my arm. I won't be able to do anything, and my agent's an ass. He's going to yell at me when he hears about this." She turned her tear-stained face to him, and Del hadn't been prepared for the rage storming through him at the thought of someone hurting Lilly.

"I'm unemployed. How will I pay for Daisy's tuition? She'll yell, too, and she's got a really mean mouth." Lilly was fisting the cloth covering the table she was sitting on, and from the look of the fabric, the hospital's staff was going to have their work cut out for them getting out the creases.

"You won't have to deal with her, love. We'll take care of it. How does that sound, Beautiful?" Del understood he was walking a fine line between Lilly's informed consent and too drugged to know what was up from down, but he rationalized it as simply doing whatever it took to calm her down.

Dean wrapped his arm around her shoulders easing her back on to the pillow. Lilly's eyes fluttered closed, and her breathing evened out, indicating she'd finally succumbed to the medication. When Cal tilted his head toward the hall, Del nodded and followed him out into the busy passageway.

"We'll have her ready to go as soon as we double-check to make sure the bones are still properly aligned after casting. From what little I got from Brayden, I assume you'd be more comfortable taking her out one of the less public exits." Del gave Cal a brief overview and watched as the other man's expression darkened. "I'll ask Dennis to coordinate with a car service, that will be safer and hopefully keep the asshat trying to locate her from tracking you to the airport."

Del appreciated Cal's help because the less time he spent on logistics was that much more time he could spend with Lilly.

THE BED RUMBLING beneath her cheek made Lilly want to shove a pillow under her head and sink back into the darkness. *When did I get on a plane? I was in New York with Del and Dean... then I remember a doctor talking about casts. Ahhhh.* The scream she'd thought was in her head bounced around her and before she could raise her arm, firm hands wrapped around her upper arm stilling her attempt to move.

"I've got you, Darlin', hold still before you hurt yourself." As Dean's words registered so did the pain. When she groaned and tried to curl into a ball, she realized her leg felt like it was encased in concrete, and the white-hot flash of pain made her eyes fill with tears.

"I heard her shout, so I brought her medicine." She saw Del step through a doorway and confusion temporarily pushed the pain to the side.

"Wait. There's a bed on this jet? I've never seen a bed on a plane before."

"This is our corporate jet, Beautiful. We enjoy our creature comforts when we travel. There are actually two bedrooms—this is the larger of the two."

She knew she was staring at Del as if he were speaking a foreign language, but she had so many questions tumbling around in her head she didn't even know where to start.

"Ordinarily, I love that dazed look in a woman's eyes because it means we've done everything right, but since I know yours is a combination of pain and genuine confusion, it's not particularly enjoyable."

She watched him move to her side and hold out two capsules, but when she started to reach for them, her arm wouldn't move.

"No, baby, let us help." Del slipped the capsules between her lips and Dean held the glass for her to drink. Lilly didn't usually take pain medications because it acted like truth serum for her, so if they were going to ask questions, she hoped they did it before the drugs took her mouth hostage.

"We'll help you to the restroom, Darlin', but then we want you back in bed before you eat anything." When she started to roll to the side of the bed, Dean shook his head. "Sweetness, you can't put any weight on your leg for at least three weeks, and with your arm in a cast, you can't use crutches." The reality of her situation slammed into her like someone had dropped a boulder on her chest.

"How am I going to... well, how am I going to do anything? Hell, I can't even go to the bathroom. My apartment isn't huge, but it's going to be hard to hop around the space." Damn, she couldn't even manage a wheelchair by herself. For a fleeting moment, Lilly wondered if her sister would stay with her and help, but the thought evaporated into a fine mist almost as quickly as it had formed. *You know she isn't going to help, don't even ask... that way you won't be hurt when she says no.*

Del slipped his arms under her legs and behind her back, lifting her effortlessly from the bed before she could protest. Moving into a surprisingly large bathroom, the two of them helped her use the restroom. Despite her protests she could manage alone, they refused to leave her unattended, insisting not only was she dealing with the after-effects of a serious accident and painkillers, she wasn't factoring in the fact everything around her was moving—fast.

"It wouldn't be safe to leave you alone, Beautiful. We already made that mistake once today, and we don't plan to repeat it." The second part had been spoken much quieter, but she hadn't missed it. Cupping her hand along his jaw, Lilly drew his attention to her.

"This isn't your fault. I'm not sure why that man wanted to hurt me, but if you'd been close, we'd have all been hurt. What kind of pickle would we be in, then? Who would be helping me right now?" There was a tenderness in his eyes that made her heart skip a beat, but there was also knowledge—and between one breath and the next, she realized he knew why she'd been targeted. Stiffening her spine, she looked between the two of them. "Tell me." Both men nodded once and moved her back into the bedroom.

"We'll explain while you eat." She wasn't sure where the tray of food had come from while they were in the bathroom, but she was grateful whoever made the tray had cut up all the fruit and cheese, so everything was easy for her to eat with one hand. She knew they'd purposely stalled, letting her eat part of the meal before they offered the explanation. *Which tells me they don't think I'll want to eat after I hear what they have to say.*

Dean was overly attentive, Del was quickly becoming uncomfortable, and Lilly was tired of pussy-footing around. "I'm a big girl, you know, and I'd appreciate it if you would just spit it out." Dean's sweet smile and gentle kiss told her as much as Del's reluctant nod. What followed was five of the hardest minutes of Lilly's life.

Suck it up, Lilly, you asked to be treated like an adult, and they've simply honored your request.

DEL COULDN'T RECALL a time when he'd hated a conversation as much as he'd hated the one he'd just finished. Lilly had known whatever was coming was going to be bad, but he was convinced she hadn't expected the level of betrayal her sister had displayed. Her emotions played out over her face in living color. Confusion... shock... fear... anger... sadness... and finally, resignation. It had all been there, and Del was confident they could deal with the fall-out, but it broke his heart she was being forced to deal with so much at one time.

"I'll make arrangements for help as soon as I get home. It won't be safe for you to be there. If I have someone come in once a day to cook, I can probably get by until I get a walking cast." *Probably? Is she fucking kidding?*

"No." Del would have laughed at the shocked look on her face if he hadn't been so frustrated with her for thinking she could get by with someone cooking one meal a day.

"No? What do you mean, no? No, I don't need help, or no, you don't feel it's unsafe?"

"Darlin', I don't think you understand the danger you're in. If the thugs who ran over you in New York show up at your front door, how would you defend yourself? Are you willing to put yourself and those who live around you at risk?"

Watching her process Dean's words, Del knew she was fighting to regain some emotional balance. Hell, she'd had her world turned upside down in a matter of a few hours, but he wasn't going to allow her damned sister to further endanger her.

"Beautiful, we meant it when we said you were ours. It's our privilege to take care of you. It would be irresponsible for us to drop you off at your house without any consideration for your safety."

"Not to mention we'd be lonely as hell without you. We wouldn't be able to concentrate on work, our business holdings would suffer, we'd have to lay off employees. That's an enormous burden, Darlin', you sure you want to put yourself through all that?" Del could only shake his head at his brother's antics, but he was grateful for the smile he saw curving Lilly's lips.

Her eyelids were drooping, and Del knew they only had a few minutes before she was fast asleep again, so he leaned forward to brush away the last tear from her flushed cheek. He didn't want her falling asleep on an emotional edge. He was dead serious when he told her she was theirs to care for—and that included her emotional well-being as well as her physical safety.

"There are two things I want you to remember, Beautiful. First, none of this is your fault. Your sister has made numerous mistakes, but the ultimate blame is on the man driving the car." As far as Del was concerned the asshole had painted a large target on his own back when he aimed the SUV at Lilly. "The second thing I want you to hold close to your heart as you fall asleep is we aren't walking away." A tear breached her lower lid and slid over her cheek. Thumbing it away, he smiled into her rapidly fading expression.

"I fell in love with you the moment our eyes met, and every moment since has strengthened the way I feel, Beautiful. I'll let my brother speak for himself, but I assure you, we're of a like mind. We've looked for you for a very long time, Love, and we have no intention of letting you slip through our fingers."

"I might have been a few beats behind my brother, but that doesn't mean my love isn't as strong, Darlin'. You are ours." Dean's simple declaration seemed to be enough to put her mind to rest. It was important she knew they were both committed to her despite the short amount of time they'd been together.

"It doesn't always take weeks, months, or years to recognize when something is right. Just because something occurs quickly doesn't make it less significant." Del had never believed in love at first sight until Lilly.

"I know I'm going to have to step away from my sister and knowing you are standing beside me gives me more strength than you can possibly know. I've fallen in love with both of you, but I don't think you'll believe me until there aren't drugs involved." Del was surprised by her insight. She was right, it would be difficult to believe the words until they were spoken with a clear head.

"Someday, many years from now, we're going to remind you of this moment—and who said it first." Del was relieved to see her relax. He'd wanted to cut through some of the tension before she slipped back into sleep. "You need to rest, Beautiful. Your body needs sleep to heal."

"One of us will stay with you at all times, Darlin'. We don't want you trying to move around without help." Dean's words had barely crossed his lips when she gave them a sleepy nod as her eyes closed.

Del would bet she hadn't fully registered Dean's warning, so they'd need to be vigilant until she understood they were serious about seeing to her well-being. Slipping from the bed, Del paced the small space several times before turning his attention to his brother.

Fucking perfect. Damned if Dean wasn't sleeping as soundly as Lilly. He'd leave them be for now, but as soon as they were back at the ranch, he planned to fuck her senseless, then tuck her against his side and get some much-needed rest. *Let my damned brother deal with business for a change while I enjoy our woman.*

He'd already made all the arrangements to pay Daisy's tuition, all the young woman had to do was promise she wouldn't contact her sister for anything money related again. Their attorney had also suggested a clause preventing Daisy from giving interviews about Lilly, so they'd added that as well. Del had the paperwork sent to Brayden, knowing how persuasive he could be. The club owner would get the paperwork signed and send it via a courier to Texas. Hell, they'd likely have it in their hands before Daisy's commercial flight landed.

Chuckling to himself as he walked out of the bedroom, he couldn't help smiling because if he had to guess, Del bet Brayden hadn't been particularly concerned when booking her flight. She probably had connections at every small airport between New York and Texas.

Chapter Thirteen

Six Weeks Later

L ILLY FLINCHED WHEN the doctor switched on the saw. She knew her eyes were wide as any kid the gentleman had ever dealt with, his genial chuckle more from experience than amusement.

"It's going to tickle, but I want you to hold still. There's a guard preventing the blade from touching your skin, but nothing protecting me, so I'd appreciate your cooperation."

Sneaky man, he'd know exactly how to get her to hold still. She'd seen Dr. Welby regularly since moving into the West's riverside mansion at the edge of Austin. They might refer to it as a ranch, but she wasn't fooled by the downplay. Del and Dean had coddled her for the past six weeks, rarely leaving her alone for longer than a few minutes at a time. She'd fallen deeper in love with them every day.

Looking up at the doctor, Lilly couldn't help but smile, remembering the first time they'd met. He'd immediately reminded her of Robert Young, and when he'd introduced himself as Dr. Welby, she'd laughed out loud. He'd grinned and shaken his head. "I don't usually get that reaction from my younger patients, many of them are too young to remember the television show." The sweet man admitted the popular series had made him the butt of more jokes than he cared to remember during medical school.

When she'd reminded him the television doctor was decades older, both Del and Dean had growled their disapproval. Their less than subtle response was the only time she'd heard Dr. Welby laugh out loud. As the saw whirled, Lilly felt her stomach turn over and instinctively pressed her hand over it, hoping she didn't embarrass herself by losing what little breakfast she'd been able to get down.

She wasn't sure where she'd picked up the bug she'd been dealing with the past few days since she rarely left the West brother's property and she wasn't alone then, and neither of the men had mentioned feeling under the weather. Lilly had promised herself she'd make some calls to agents when she got back to the house, but all she could think about now was how much she wanted a nap.

"Are you all right, Darlin'? Your face is awfully pale, and I noticed you're holding your stomach again this morning." Del's observation surprised her, but she wasn't sure why... *damn, they don't miss anything.*

"I'll be fine, I think I caught a bug." She'd no sooner finished speaking than the room began spinning and her worst fears began playing out around her. Del handed her a small basin, and the doctor switched off the saw before he was finished and stood, studying her closely.

"How long have you been sick, Lilly?" When she explained she'd felt this way the past few mornings, he frowned and turned to speak quietly to the nurse who'd been standing nearby. The woman smiled at her before slipping from the room. *I hope she'd gone for a cool cloth or maybe some toast.*

Del moved behind her, straddling the table so he could pull her back against his chest. The reclining position helped, but it was his touch she found the most settling.

Sucking in several deep breaths and relaxing into Del's arms, Lilly felt better and nodded to the doctor to continue. She stayed quiet while he finished removing the cast from her leg and sighed when cool air rushed over the skin that had been covered for so long. The refreshing sensation was quickly overshadowed by a stench that had her gagging into the basin before she had a chance to swallow it back. By the time her stomach was empty, humiliation swamped her, and she felt tears fill her eyes.

"God in heaven, I just want to crawl in a hole and hide. I'm so sorry. Damn, I feel awful exposing you all to this."

"Lilly, I'm fairly certain none of us are going to *catch* it." The doctor's comments might have meant more if she'd been able to think past the sea sickness swamping her. *When did we get on a damned boat?*

DEL HAD MOVED behind Lilly so he could comfort her, but he'd also wanted to hide the smile he knew was spreading over his face. He and Dean had both been certain Lilly was pregnant, but this was the first time they'd seen any evidence beyond the changes in her body. They hadn't mentioned it to her in case they'd been wrong, but he was certain the jig was about to be up.

Smiling to himself, Del remembered the night they'd proposed to her. They'd planned everything in excruciating detail even including her new passion for the firing range into a day centered around all her favorite things. He was continually amazed at how quickly she'd become proficient with the small firearms they'd gotten her, particularly considering she was using her non-dominant hand. He was more than a bit worried about how good she'd be once she could use her right hand again.

After a day spent "blowing things up" as she liked to refer to it, they'd settled under the stars along the river with wine, cheese, and bread. When darkness finally settled around them, thousands of fairy lights sparkled from the trees. They'd hired local college kids to string the lights, then focused their attention on keeping their observant sub from spotting the fun-loving group.

The students had been thrilled to earn money for their drama group, and when Dean treated them to a pizza party after they'd finished, they'd offered to come back to help decorate for the wedding. At first, he and Del had laughed at their lighting suggestions, but the more they listened, the more interested they'd become. Lilly had been enchanted by the lights and laughed when she heard how they'd managed to decorate with so many lights in such a short amount of time.

"It looks like a fairy wonderland. I thought perhaps you'd finally found my fairy godmother... heaven knows the old bat hides from me every chance she gets. I always figured Daisy was scaring her away, but now I'm starting to think she's forced to work so hard, she collapses in exhaustion." Dean asked her what she'd meant, and even in the dim light, Del had seen her blush. "The day we met, Daisy had wanted to eat at a place across the street, but when we'd walked by the café where you found me sitting, I felt as if I was being drawn inside. The maître d' tried to seat is in the center of the room because he'd recognized me, but I wanted to be by the windows."

"Let me guess. You convinced him you'd be more visible there." Del laughed out loud when she gasped in surprise. "Don't look so surprised, Beautiful. You were absolutely right, and we'll thank our lucky stars every night for the rest of our lives he listened." It was the truth, he and Dean knew they were blessed, and now it looked as though they had another blessing on the way.

The three of them had only had one disagreement. Lilly had been livid they'd paid for Daisy's education. She'd insisted they shouldn't have wasted their hard-earned money on the ungrateful wench, but Del still believed it was money well spent because the agreement was keeping Daisy away from Lilly. It hadn't taken Brayden's staff long to get the word out on the street the goons who'd targeted Lilly had gotten the wrong woman. Brayden's claim Lilly's identification had been stolen by her certifiably insane sister had been a bonus as far as Del was concerned.

Sliding their ring on her finger and hearing her say yes to their heartfelt proposals had been one of the best moments of Del's life, and he knew Dean felt the same. They'd talked about the future, and she'd told them she wanted to wait until after her casts were removed to get married so she could step out of Charlie and Dollie's carriage and walk up the aisle without the walking cast clomping with every step she took.

"We have waited for you for so long, I'm not going to be willing to wait much longer before knowing you belong to us in every way possible. Don't forget, the doctor warned you it would be a long time before you'll be able to wear your stilettos." Dr. Welby had pulled him aside and warned him the sky-high heels were going to be painful and dangerous for a good long while. The doctor suggested hiding her collection, but they'd simply cautioned her against doing any further damage.

Holding her now, feeling her relax in his arms sent a wave of contentment through Del he hadn't expected. The nurse stepped back into the room holding a small tray with a few crackers and a can of Sprite. Lilly looked relieved, but when she reached for them, Dean shook his head and fed her small bites and sips of the soda. She seemed to be settling before the second cast opened, and she gasped at the peeling skin revealed. Damn it, he'd intended to distract her but was so lost in the feel of her in his embrace, he'd forgotten.

A young man drew blood from her arm, but Lilly was so focused on Dean's teasing with the crackers and drink, she'd barely registered the needle piercing her arm. Dr. Welby cleaned her arm, encouraged her to keep the physical therapy appointments he'd set up for her and chatted for several minutes before another nurse handed him a folded piece of paper.

"Congratulations, Lilly, you're going to be a mother. I'll be happy to recommend an obstetrician unless you have someone in mind." It wasn't until she failed to respond, Del realized she'd stopped breathing. Leaning forward, he brushed his lips over her ear.

"Breathe, Love. Our baby needs oxygen, and so does his sweet mama." He tried to temper his voice, but it was hard to hide joy. He felt her take a deep breath and saw his brother smiling like the cat who'd caught the canary. The doctor chuckled and shook his head.

"It never gets old seeing that stunned look in a woman's eyes when she first hears she's going to have a baby. You'll start feeling better in a few weeks, Lilly, but until then, the nurse is gathering some information for you, including some tricks that might help you fend off the worst of the nausea. Be sure you mention these symptoms to your OB.

LILLY KNEW SHE was staring at the man as if he was speaking a foreign language, but honest to God, that was exactly how it felt. With just a few words he'd tilted her entire world so far off-center, she might well have tumbled off the exam table if Del hadn't been holding her. Nothing he said was fully registering, and she'd already stopped breathing once, causing concerned looks on the faces of the two men in front of her.

There had been a small part of her that had dreaded the day she'd have to leave Del and Dean to return to work. Now that work was going to be delayed for at least a year, she suddenly felt surprisingly insecure about staying.

What if they didn't want to be fathers? Damn, what if they wanted to know which one of them *was* the father? She didn't want to come between them and putting that burden on a child was equally unacceptable. Chewing on her lip, Lilly watched the black dots begin dancing in her vision again and wondered why they were growing larger.

Mother. I don't know how to be a mother. Hell, my own mother wasn't even a mother. She and my father might be biologically responsible for me, but they've never seen me as anything other than a financial burden. Lilly had overhead them arguing one night and knew they'd both been disappointed they hadn't had sons, but by that time she was immune to their disinterest.

"Lilly, you'll be a wonderful mother, and we're thrilled you're carrying our child." Dean's use of her name captured her attention, and she sucked in a deep breath, trying to focus on his face. "The only thing this changes is how quickly we make our commitment legal. We'd always planned to do whatever it took to keep you, Darlin'."

When she blinked at him in surprise, he chuckled. "I know that look, sweetness and you can push that thought right on out of your head."

Del gave her a quick squeeze from behind, then slowly moved until he was standing beside her. Del pushed his fingers into her hair, stroke after stroke, massaging her scalp before combing through the long strands all the way to the end.

"We would have never stood in the way of your career, Beautiful. We want to enhance your life, not micromanage it." Pressing a lingering kiss to her lips until she felt herself starting to relax. "Let's get you home, little mama. You start physical therapy tomorrow, and we've got wedding plans to make." Lilly started to move from the table, but Dean lifted her into his arms before she could get to her feet.

"Speaking from experience, Darlin', you will want to start out nice and slow, putting weight on your ankle is not going to be as easy as it seems. I swore a blue streak when I jumped off the table in my doctor's office after he'd cut the cast off my leg."

"He cried like a damned baby and begged them to put the cast back on. It was embarrassing." Del winked at her over his brother's shoulder, and Lilly was grateful for the laughter. That simple exchange was all it took to break the dam that had been holding back her joy, and she was suddenly overwhelmed with emotion. Both men looked horrified at the sudden shift. Their panicked expressions made her heart squeeze with love.

"I'm the luckiest girl in the whole world. I'm not sure you know what you're getting into, but I promise to make sure your life is never dull. Now, can we go to the range and blow up something?"

Epilogue

LILLY FELT LIKE she was swimming through clear gelatin. The damned stuff was thick enough to blur her vision and muffle sound, but she could still see the surface. Knowing the way out and getting there were proving to be very different things. The surface was a pinpoint of light up ahead, but she was already exhausted and still had so far to go she wasn't sure she'd make it.

Shivering as the air shifted around her, Lilly wanted to cry with relief when someone's warm hand wrapped around her much colder one. The masculine voice was familiar and filled with compassion as he pleaded with her to return to them. Before she had time to wonder who else was waiting for her, another warm hand stroked the side of her face. The gesture was so comforting, Lilly felt herself relax knowing there were people nearby to pull her to the surface if she ran out of steam.

"Come on, Beautiful, we're waiting for you to return to us. Dean and I are here, but the waiting room is filled with everyone who loves you."

"They're all waiting for us to tell them you're awake and giving us a run for our money, Darlin'. You don't want to disappoint your sons, do you?"

"Tobi is threatening to take the hospital apart if you aren't treated like royalty, so I'm sure the staff would appreciate your cooperation, as well." This time there was more amusement in his tone, and her heart skipped a beat when she realized the men speaking to her were the husbands she'd been terrified she'd never see again.

The last thing she remembered was seeing the horrified expression on a young woman's face when she looked up from her phone a split second before she'd struck Lilly's new car dead center in the front passenger door. Lilly remembered worrying about how Del and Dean would react to her crashing the new vehicle even as the impact was sending her head crashing against the driver's window.

As the sound of breaking glass and twisting metal filled her ears, Lilly had heard a woman screaming her husbands' names and wondered as darkness was closing in around her how the desperate sounding lady knew her charming men.

She opened her mouth to ask about the other driver, but her throat was so dry, she couldn't get any sound to come out. There were murmurs around her, then something cold and wet painted her parched lips, making her sigh her thanks. Before she could speak, a high-pitched voice sounded from somewhere in the distance.

"Lilly West is my mother in every way that matters. Stand between us... try to keep me from going in to check on her, and I will take your grumpy ass out. I may be smaller than you, but I'm damned mean when you try to keep me from the people I love." Lilly's eyes finally fluttered open in time to see the woman she loved with her entire heart shove her way into the room.

"See? She's awake, and you were trying to keep me out. You should be ashamed of yourself." Lilly felt her heart lighten when she heard her son grumbling about disrespectful subs you can't take out in public. Tobi was at her side two seconds later, big tears rolling unchecked down her pale cheeks. "You've taken a decade off my life.

This is proof I'm never going to survive my children learning to drive."

"Come on, Sweetness. Let the dads spend time with Mom. We'll come back when she's had a chance to get her bearings. You promised you'd go home and rest as soon as you knew she was awake." Kent led Tobi toward the door, but before they disappeared into what Lilly assumed was the hall, she turned, and Lilly could see the younger woman was barely holding herself together.

"Thank you for coming back to us. I know what it's like to want to give up, and I'm so grateful you didn't give in to the temptation. Thank you for choosing us."

The End

Books by Avery Gale

The ShadowDance Club
Katarina's Return – Book One
Jenna's Submission – Book Two
Rissa's Recovery – Book Three
Trace & Tori – Book Four
Reborn as Bree – Book Five
Red Clouds Dancing – Book Six
Perfect Picture – Book Seven

Club Isola
Capturing Callie – Book One
Healing Holly – Book Two
Claiming Abby – Book Three

Masters of the Prairie Winds Club
Out of the Storm
Saving Grace
Jen's Journey
Bound Treasure
Punishing for Pleasure
Accidental Trifecta
Missionary Position
Another Second Chance
Star-Crossed Miracles
Dusted Star
Lilly's Choice

The Wolf Pack Series
Mated – Book One
Fated Magic – Book Two
Tempted by Darkness – Book Three

The Knights of the Boardroom
Book One
Book Two
Book Three

The Morgan Brothers of Montana
Coral Hearts – Book One
Dancing with Deception – Book Two
Caged Songbird – Book Three
Game On – Book Four
Well Bred – Book Five

Mountain Mastery
Well Written
Savannah's Sentinel
Sheltering Reagan

The Christmas Painting

I would love to hear from you!

Website:
www.averygalebooks.com/index.html

Facebook:
facebook.com/avery.gale.3

Twitter:
@avery_gale